THE GROUNDSKEEPER

A NOVEL BY

Colton Evers

PublishAmerica
Baltimore

© 2008 by Colton Evers.
All rights reserved. No part of this book may be reproduced, stored in a retrieval system or transmitted in any form or by any means without the prior written permission of the publishers, except by a reviewer who may quote brief passages in a review to be printed in a newspaper, magazine or journal.

First printing

All characters in this book are fictitious, and any resemblance to real persons, living or dead, is coincidental.

PublishAmerica has allowed this work to remain exactly as the author intended, verbatim, without editorial input.

ISBN: 1-60672-540-8
PUBLISHED BY PUBLISHAMERICA, LLLP
www.publishamerica.com
Baltimore

Printed in the United States of America

I Envy the Wind

It Has No Memory

Of Where It's Been

INTRODUCTION

We were heading north on Highway Thirty-Five, driving under cover of darkness. A light rain had begun to fall. I looked over at him and could tell he was very tense. He kept turning to look behind. A loud crack of thunder was followed by large drops pelting the windshield. I leaned over and turned the radio on. How fitting. The song that began to play was "Rider's on the Storm."

As I listened to the words I watched him out of the corner of my eye. Some of the lines in the song troubled me. What if he isn't the person I believe him to be? Could he be as the song said, "A killer on the road?" Another cold chill greeted me as the song continued with, "If you give this man a ride sweet family will die."

Suddenly, out of nowhere, headlights appeared right behind us. I slowed to let them pass but they stuck right on my tail. Was it them? How could they have found us so fast?

It can't end like this! It just can't. Not after all that's happened in the past weeks.

Chapter One

Three weeks earlier

The morning started out like every other morning. My alarm clock went off, I went into denial that it was 6 a.m., and the dog was barking. Even though it was Tuesday it felt like a Monday.

I sat on the edge of my bed looking at my calendar. There it was; May 18th, 1999 only nineteen days to go. Finally I would be done with School. Over! Finished! With that recharging thought I went about getting ready for my day, which included school, work, and of course, Lily.

I arrived at the school about twenty minutes early, parking my car carefully at the end of the parking lot, and sat down to enjoy the morning sun. The sun can be so rewarding at this time in the morning, beaming down on your face, creating a warmth and freshness that can be best absorbed by leaning your head back and shutting your eyes.

My peaceful moments were short lived. I could hear shouting and loud laughter. Some of the guys were running behind the old man that looks after the grounds. He was on a riding lawnmower cutting the lawn minding his own business, but they were running up behind him shouting and trying to scare him. Such idiots! The old man was deaf, and he couldn't even hear them. Now they were running up to him and pushing him, then roaring with laughter, no doubt trying to impress the girls nearby, who shared in the laughter. This was going too far. They wouldn't quit

I decided to make it my business. I couldn't stand the old man being subjected to this cruel treatment. I stood up and yelled at them to leave the man alone, he wasn't bothering anyone. That was all it took for me to come up with a recipe for disaster. The whole group of them came over to me. Their ringleader and spokesman walked up to me and stops about two inches from my nose and says, "What's it to you punk?"

"Just leave the old man alone. The guys deaf for God's sake, show a little respect."

He gave me a two handed shove that almost knocked me to the ground. Now I had to make one of those spur of the moment decisions, and being that self-control was never one of my strong points, I hauled off and slugged him square on the nose.

Well that's all it took. He hit the ground and was down for the count. It took exactly a split second for his three cronies to react. They came at me all at once. I definitely was not going to gain the upper hand. In short order I was on the ground, and the three were joined by their bloody nosed pal, all determined to put out my lights.

Just as things were starting to look very bleak, the guys were being hauled off of me, one by one. I scrambled to get up to see what was happening. I stood there in disbelief. The old man had pulled these guys off of me and part of my disbelief included the look on the old man's face as the four idiots stood there. The look he gave them was a deep, cold stare, very cold. Who would have thought he could affect them that much.

They weren't going to mess with this guy, cowards that they were. They offered the lame excuse that they had to get to class. Off they went, yelling obscenities, which the old man couldn't hear anyway.

Well, talk about the unexpected, and I might add, very impressive. And to think that in all the years I had attended this high school, I'd never given this man a second thought.

THE GROUNDSKEEPER

As I stood there, I realized I should at least thank him. He had walked back to his riding lawnmower he had been cutting the lawn with. So I called out to him, "Hey, thanks a lot."

I had no sooner said it, than it hit me as to what an idiot I was. The guy's deaf. So I ran over and came around to the front of the riding mower just as he was starting it. We made eye contact and in a slow, deliberate manner I said, "Thank you."

He watched my lips as I spoke, and when I was finished he gave me a smile, nodded his head, then raised his right hand and gave me a thumbs up signal. I smiled back and felt good that he had understood what I said. He put the mower in gear and continued with his work. I stood there for a few minutes, just watching him. I wasn't sure why, but there was something different about him. Any other time he had been working on the grounds, or around the school, it was like he didn't exist. But today was different, maybe because I've always fought my own battles, and never had anyone lend a hand like he did. I realized here was a man that deserved respect.

For the rest of the day I found it hard to concentrate on school. This wasn't uncommon, though, as I usually spent my time thinking about that special girl of mine, Lily, my car, and basketball. But today it was the groundskeeper. I wondered how old he actually was, what it would be like going through life as a dear mute, and of course, what is his name?

I came up with a plan. After school I got into my car and drove over to Stanton High, where Lily attended. Their classes ended fifteen minutes after ours. I pulled into the parking lot in the usual place I would wait for her. A few minutes later she came out and over to the car.

"Hi Lily, how are you?" I asked.

"Good thanks," she answered, leaning over to look at the marks on my face as she got in the car.

"Quint, I'm afraid to ask" she said, shaking her head. "Did you have a game today?"

"No, just a little encounter with a collection of idiots."

"So tell me, what happened?"

"Never mind that right now, I've got something real important I want to ask you."

Her face lit up with anticipation, then came back to the norm as I asked;

"Didn't you tell me that your great great-grandfather taught sign language and your grandmother taught you some too?"

A puzzled look came over Lily as she answered, "Yes, but why in the world are you asking me that for?"

I told Lily what had happened today, and that I wanted to try to communicate with the old guy who looked after the grounds. Lily thought it was a very kind thing to do, and would try to help me with some basic signing, but admitted she was very limited in what she actually knew and understood. Nevertheless, this was a starting point. We drove off to her house, sat in the back yard, she explained how to greet in sign language, and taught me how to ask what his name was.

However I had a question, "If he answers me in sign, and tries to tell me his name, I'll never be able to figure it out."

"That's no problem," Lily answered. "Because all you have to do is bring a pen and writing pad, and he can write it out for you right there."

"Well come to think of it, why don't I just write my questions on a piece of paper and just let him write out the answers?"

"You could, but usually if a deaf mute sees you're putting forth an effort to use Sign Language, they're more likely to open up to you."

"Good point, as usual. I should learn to listen more to you."

That evening Lily and I drove around for a couple of hours

with the top down on my convertible. Around nine I stopped to drop her off at home, gave her a kiss, and told her I'd see her after school tomorrow. Lily hesitated for a moment as she was about to get out of the car. I knew she had something on her mind. She looked at me and asked, "Have you thought anymore about my dad's offer to work at his plant?"

I thought carefully about my response. I sure didn't want to hurt Lily. She was trying very hard to get me to change my mind about careers. I wasn't upset about it, I knew she really cared, and was looking out for my best interests. I looked at her, she was so beautiful, and I knew this was the person I wanted to spend the rest of my life with, and I needed to be gentle about my response.

"I've thought about this most every day. Honestly, I haven't decided yet. I know you don't care for the idea of the police academy. I know you said it scares you but please remember all those statistics sometimes paint the picture too black."

"Quint, you know I do love you very much. I just don't want anything to happen to you."

"Thanks sweetheart, I love you too, very much. I know how you feel about this whole business, and I'll talk to you more about it, but right now I've got to get to the shop because we're doing inventory tonight. I'll see you tomorrow for sure."

I drove off thinking how lucky I was to have a girl like Lily. She was one in a million, and I knew that soon I would have to decide about careers.

The next morning I pulled into the school parking lot and carefully parked my car as always, on an angle in the last parking spot, so no dumb moron would ding my car when opening their car door. I scanned the grounds to see if the old guy was anywhere in sight, but there was no sign of him. I went into the school to my first class. As lunch hour arrived I went to sit outside to see if I could catch sight of him. No sign of him, so I walked around the school to see if he was working on the other side.

COLTON EVERS

Sure enough there he was trimming the cedar hedges by the back entrance to the school. He was very engrossed in his work, so I decided to sit on the back steps to see if he would catch sight of me, instead of me going up to him and startling him. I had been sitting for about five minutes when he caught sight of me looking at him from the steps. He gave me that nod with his head and motioned with his hand, which I guessed was somewhat of a greeting, then continued with his work. Well at least we were acknowledging one another. But I still wanted to at least know his name. I walked over to him and he saw me coming. Even though I was smiling, he had a very serious look on his face; an uneasiness. I quickly began to use the sign language Lily had showed me. As clumsy as I must have looked, I do think my greeting amused him, and he must have understood it because he smiled a wide smile, almost as if he was about to laugh. Needless to say I didn't feel real intelligent, but then he reached out his right hand to me and I realized he wanted to shake my hand.

All right, I thought. Feeling quite pleased with myself, I put my hand out to shake his. As we shook hands I thought to myself, this guy has true grip, something that's a lot better than shaking some guy's soft wimpy hand. And to boot he looked me straight in the eyes.

As I looked at him I felt his eyes had a penetrating characteristic about them. But hey, no problem, maybe the other senses are making up for what he lacks in speech and hearing. He then turned and got back to his work.

Wait, I thought, I didn't get his name. Then I realized I hadn't brought my pen and writing pad with me. So I rushed back to the school, but by this time the bell had rung for next class. I'd have to wait until later for another chance to get his name.

Little did I know that my efforts this day would set in motion

THE GROUNDSKEEPER

a series of events that no one would have ever imagined. This groundskeeper was about to add new meaning to the saying, "Things are not always what they appear to be."

Chapter Two

As soon as school was over I went out to look for the groundskeeper, before I was going to head over to Stanton High to pick up Lily. Again, he was no where in sight so I walked over to the parking lot to get my car.

Much to my horror, the same collection of idiots I had the run in with yesterday, were all leaning against my car. I knew there was a very slim chance of a peaceful way to deal with this. But for the sake of my car, I may have to eat some crow, and let these guys feel they've got the upper hand. As I came within a few feet of the car, their ringleader Chris, leaned over the hood of my car, and pulled a long nail out of his pocket.

"Just thought maybe I'd carve my initials on the hood scoop of this baby," he said with a sarcastic smirk, as he looked over to his buddies.

So much for any thought of a peaceful outcome. I snapped at him; "You touch the car, and I'll break every finger on both your hands!"

"Oh boy! Tough guy eh?"

There was no doubt in my mind that I was going to put my car first ahead of anything. That meant I had to get the old girl out of here. I slowly reached for my keys, as I planned a dash for the driver's seat, firing the old girl up and vacating. Then, some more of the unexpected!

I couldn't believe it! I didn't even see him coming! But there

THE GROUNDSKEEPER

he was, standing at the other side of the car, none other than the groundskeeper! Now that he had everyone's attention, he slowly walked to the front of the car, and right up to Chris, who was no longer leaning over the hood. All the while he kept one hand behind his back.

As might be expected, Chris synonymous with big mouth, piped up with, "What do you want old man?"

Obviously, he wasn't going to answer, but his next move removed all doubt as to what he was made of. It spoke a lot louder than any words could have. Much to my surprise, and yet very much to my delight, he pulled a baseball bat from behind his back. Yes, nothing like a good three foot piece of Hickory! At this point Chris was visibly uncomfortable, as the groundskeeper kept up an intense glaring stare at him. Without even blinking, and of course without a word, he was holding the bat in his left hand, and began to tap it gently on the palm of his right hand. He kept this up for about twenty seconds, still not breaking his stare, then Chris, trying to salvage what little nerve he had, says, "You ain't worth it old man!" With that he motioned to his fellow idiots to leave. Chris turned and asked, "What the hell kind of name is Quint anyway?"

I thought I'd seize the moment, and replied with, "Sure a lot more masculine than a name like Chrissy." I knew now I had made another friend for life.

Now back to reality. Wow, that was close! My old girl would have probably been marked up pretty bad if it weren't for this guy. This was the second time in two days that he came to my rescue, and I still didn't even know his name. I walked up to him and again said thank you, in a slow deliberate way. He gave me a smile, and a nod, and turned to leave. Instantly I reached out to grab a hold of his arm, so he wouldn't leave. He turned quickly and looked at me with a very cold look. Immediately I said, "I'm sorry!"

His cold look eased up. I told him, "I don't even know your name."

Here I was trying to talk to him, and he's deaf. To my surprise though, he must have read my lips, because he reached into his shirt pocket, and pulled out a card. It looked like a business card, but when he handed it to me it realized that this is what he shows people who don't realize he's deaf. The card said, "My name is William E. Brown. Please call me Web. I am a deaf mute, but can read lips. Thank you."

Web. That's pretty neat I thought, as I handed back the card to him. We both exchanged smiles. It felt good. When he took the card back, he took a pen from his pocket and wrote something on the back of the card. He handed it back to me. I read it, and it asked my name. I wrote Quint Matthews on the card and handed it back. Then he took out a small writing pad and wrote something else. He handed it to me, and I read it. It brought a special kind of smile. He had written, "Nice Car." I thought to myself, here's a guy who must have an appreciation for true Detroit Muscle; the '70 Chevelle, 454.

I was feeling a depth of gratitude for what he had done for me today, and about all I could do in return was to extend my hand to shake his. He really had a firm handshake to go along with what seemed to be an inner strength, one that Chris and his fellow idiots were afraid of. He left right after the hand shake, but as he walked off, I felt for some strange reason I would like to get to know him better. It was odd for me to feel that way, because I've never been drawn to people. But Web, seemed, well, very different.

Over the next few days I decided not to bring my car to school, so as to reduce the risk of damage. It was a short walk to school anyway, and I needed the exercise. Whenever I would see him working around the school, he would acknowledge me with a wave and a nod of his head. I wanted so much to get to know him better, but I sensed he needed his space, and didn't want it invaded. I could respect that I thought; I'm no different.

A few days later, during lunch hour, I was sitting out on one of the benches in front of the school. Web was on the east side of the school yard picking up some debris at street edge of the school property. I could see a Police Cruiser slowing down, and noticed that as the Cruiser came closer, Web turned his back to the road, and slowly walked toward the school, picking up garbage as he went. The Police Cruiser slowly moved on, but I did think it was strange how Web may have turned away intentionally, or maybe it was just a coincidence. My suspicious nature was showing.

I finished my lunch, and still had a few minutes before class. Web had gone around to the side of the school where the tool shed, or his office as maybe it should be called, was located. Thinking that he's probably in there, I should pay him a visit. After all, even if he needs his space, I hadn't had any contact with him for days, so maybe now would be a good time. I went to the tool shed and knocked on the door. Then realizing that was another dumb move, how was he going to hear it? Then I noticed the bell on the side of the door, so I rang it. The door opened and there was Web. He smiled and to my surprise, motioned for me to come in.

Interesting place I thought. It was neat, clean, and had lots of pictures of old Chevys. Web motioned to the other chair, so I sat down, and admired his little retreat. I had wondered how he heard the bell, but I saw the red light bulb over his work bench, that lights up when the bell is rung. Web walked over to a small fridge, opened it and offered me a soda. I accepted, and he took one as well, and we both sat there quietly to enjoy our drink.

I kept admiring the pictures of the cars, mostly muscle cars, when Web took a piece of paper and wrote on it, "Detroit's Finest!" I shook my head in agreement especially since they were all GM products. I stood up to get a closer look, and after scanning all the beauties, I gave him the thumbs up. As I sat down I felt for him, this was really a lonely existence for him, being deaf, can't speak, and doesn't have any pictures of family or anyone on the walls. Wondering whether or not he had any family here, I took a sheet of paper and wrote out my question. He read it, and shook his head indicating no. His facial expression seemed to change, and I sensed this may be another invasion of his privacy. Then again maybe it struck a cord. Either way it was likely an invasion of sorts, a topic best left alone.

I wanted to stay but thought it might be best to take my leave. When I stood up I noticed the baseball bat leaning in the corner by his work bench. I went over and picked it up and then wrote the following on a sheet of paper, "Nothing like a good piece of hickory!" He smiled and wrote back, "Gets a lot jobs done!" I thought to myself I like the sound of that, and wrote down in response, "Unfriendly persuader," to which he seemed to get a kick out of as he very deliberately nodded in the affirmative and held up two thumbs!

I looked at my watch and pointed to the time. I had to get back to class. As I was leaving I thought it odd he had a picture of the Jack of Hearts, and the Jack of Spades on the wall. I would have to ask him one day why those two cards?

Over the next while I would stop in to see Web pretty near every day, and we communicated about cars and horsepower, and the like. It was impressive how much he knew about cars and engines, and much like myself had very little use for most of the new vehicles, which as he expressed on paper, "Have too many bell and whistles, it's a recipe for disaster." One day I asked him about the cards, the Jacks, of Hearts and Spades. He simply wrote in response, "Some day I'll tell you."

THE GROUNDSKEEPER

Finally the remaining school days had come down to the wire. I wondered what Web would be doing all summer. His answer surprised me. It also reminded me that even though you think you know someone, there's always more to find out. Web wrote on a note pad that he would be looking after the school grounds one day a week, but the rest of the time he'd be busy in his garden. I looked at him with a surprised look then thought, maybe I could come by to see it. I asked him, on the note pad if I could, and he hesitated. He looked down at the ground. My first thought was he misunderstood my question. After a few seconds he took the note pad and wrote his answer, very slowly. Why was he struggling with such a simple request? It dawned on me from previous experience in asking him things about his family maybe he felt this was another area where it invades his privacy. He handed me back the note pad where he had written, "Okay but I'll have to let you know when." I gave him the thumbs up, all the while feeling like a heel for asking. Wait. I didn't even know his address. Then again, now is probably not the time. I'd best wait until the actual end of school.

Since I was trying to steer away from questions that he might find invasive, I decided to ask him something about myself. I took the note pad and wrote, "Web, I have to make some decisions when I'm through with school. What do you think about me being a cop?" Web read my question, and with a frown on his face he wrote in capital letters, "WHY A COP?" When he finished writing he underlined the question three times pressing the pen hard on the paper. Needles to say his answer caught me off guard. I wasn't sure what to say. All I could think of was a one word answer, so I wrote, "Justice!"

Web's reaction said it all. He read my answer, shook his head, then ripped the paper from pad, and with a fury crumpled it up and threw it over into the corner. As I watched nervously, he took a deep breath, then sighed, and wrote "Sorry!" He got up and put his hand on my shoulder, biting his lip as if he had more to say. I was afraid to ask, given his violent reaction. He took the note pad, sat down, and began to write something more. He wrote for about two minutes pausing at times to think. I was anxious to read what he had to say. Finally he finished and handed me the note pad. I was about to understand him even more after this.

What he had written was this, "Justice. There is only one who can render true justice, and his is not on this earth. There is no and can be no justice in this world because even the men 'in charge' are corrupt and don't care about justice, they only care about themselves. There's too much greed and corruption in this world. Justice gets pushed into the back ground every where around the world. And on the lowest level of justice being a cop, you'll only be beating your head against the wall. You'll catch a criminal red-handed, but he's got rights. You catch a cold blooded murderer red handed, but he's got rights. You catch a serial killer, with boat loads of evidence, but he's got rights. And like all criminals they get all kinds of police protection, so nobody hurts the criminal, then they're sent to prison, get fed, clothed, receive medical care, computers, and the list goes on and on. That's Justice?"

Talk about impact. I sure hadn't expected any thing like this. This was heavy! I raised my eyes to look at him without lifting my head. I think he took it as a look of disbelief or wonderment because he took the note pad from me and started writing more. He handed it back to me. It said, "You're wondering why I say these things?" I looked up at him and shook my head in the affirmative. He motioned for me to hand back the note pad, and he continued writing. Again he handed it back to me. His answer was simple and straightforward. It read, "Because I know things!" Wow. He emphasized his answer with seven exclamation marks. I think he's trying to make a point.

THE GROUNDSKEEPER

My next thought was that I was glad I had got to know him, strange as it may seem. But today convinced me of something I felt the time he pulled those guys off of me in the schoolyard. He does command respect, there is definitely something about him, something different, and I'm not clear on what it is. I could hope that he'll let me in his world.

Chapter Three

Four days, then that's it! Four years of High School finished. However along with this milestone would also come my decision about a career. Each day I thought about how Lily felt, and how my decision would affect her. After school I was to meet her and we were going to have a burger and catch a movie, after which I knew she was going to ask me about my choice. But I had also thought a lot about what Web had said about justice. There's no doubt he has a lot more to tell than what he told me. Today I would talk to him about it some more. Who knows, maybe he might help me make a more informed decision.

I looked for Web during lunch. He wasn't in his "office" or anywhere on the grounds. I looked in the staff parking lot for his old blue pick-up, but it wasn't there. Maybe he had gone to the hardware store to pick up something for the school. As I came to the front of the school to eat my lunch, I saw Web's blue Chevy pick-up go by. He went right by the school parking lot entrance, and kept going. Strange I thought. Why wouldn't he come back to the school? Then I got a brain wave. Maybe he's going home to have lunch. With that thought in mind I rushed over to get my car, to follow him. This was my chance to find out where he lives, since I still didn't have his address.

I raced out of the school parking lot and tried to catch up to him. I came to the four way stop on Wilson Avenue and looked in all three directions, and sure enough no sign of Web's pick-up.

Well, I tried. I decided to return to the school. When I got to the next corner I turned right on Bayville Drive, and as I drove on, caught a glimpse of a blue pick-up parked by an old house. I stopped the car, and backed up so I could be sure about what looked like Web's truck. I sat there thinking, should I do this? Hey, why not! I got out of the car and walked down the driveway to the back yard. Instantly I was filled with awe.

Man-o-man, this was just like a paradise! It was beautiful. Flowers, bird baths, roses everywhere! This was amazing, talk about a green thumb! How I wished Lily could see this. In the next second I jumped near a foot off the ground! I felt this hand on my shoulder, and turned to see Web standing there. I hadn't heard him coming. However, I was more concerned about the frown on his face. I knew the look. I had invaded his privacy. But I had to tell him, pointing to the garden that it's beautiful. He simply pointed to his watch, which told me it was time to head back to school. He walked over to his truck, and I to my car, thinking; he truly is a man of few words! Driving back to school, I reasoned that he's probably quite content to have things the way they are in his life without anyone else in the picture. It disturbed me that things were working out this way, for I wanted so much to get to know him better. Perhaps, one good thing came out of today, I knew where he lived. But there would be one more good thing this day, I was to spend time with Lily.

After school I picked her up and we grabbed a take out order and drove to the lake. The lake was like glass, very calm, and a distinct stillness in the air. We stayed there until the sun started to set. I had explained to Lily what had happened at Web's house, Web being a familiar topic according to Lily.

She commented that I was always talking about him, but I think she was somewhat intrigued by him as well.

"Why do you think he didn't want you at his house?" she asked.

"The only thing I can think of is that he wants his privacy, almost total privacy."

"Yes but he let you come into his office and spend some time there."

"I know, but his home is obviously different. I'll just have to respect that."

We drove off just as the sun was setting. Lily asked me about my decision regarding the Police Force. I told her no I hadn't decided. She just smiled and then we were back to our familiar topic, Web.

"Hey," she asked, "why don't you drive by his house, I'd like to see where he lives."

"He lives on Bayville Drive, but by the time we get there it'll be dark, and you won't be able to see much."

"Well drive by any way, I just want to see where he lives. Come on."

I agreed and about ten minutes later we drove slowly down his street. The mufflers were quite loud on my car so I drove very slow, hoping as much as possible to go somewhat unnoticed. As we came up to the house, everything was dark, no lights were on. Lily said he must be asleep or out. I told her he strikes me as one of those people who are up at five a.m. and hit the sack at sunset. We continued on and I took Lily home. After I dropped her off, I again drove past his house, I wasn't really sure why. Perhaps curiosity, or maybe the chance to see him again. As before, no lights, no sign of anyone, and I couldn't even see if his truck was parked in the back. I gave my head a shake, and then realized what am I doing? Just leave and see him in the morning.

The next morning, before class, I went to Web's "office." I rang the bell and the door opened. Web smiled and motioned for me to come in. He was making coffee and offered me a cup. He was acting quite hospitable compared to yesterday. That's a relief! I took a sip of coffee, and told him, "Not Bad." He gestured with his hand as if to say, "So-So!" He reached for his writing pad and began to write something. He finished and handed me the pad. I was anxious to read what he'd written. It read, "Yesterday wasn't a good day. Sorry." I waived my hand to indicate no problem, don't worry. He smiled and appeared thankful that I understood.

At this point, now at the end of school, I wanted to bring up the police force again. I took the writing pad and wrote, "I have to decide soon about being a cop, or if I want to work for Lily's father." I handed it to Web, and as soon as he finished reading it he began to write his response. It didn't take long for him to write it. He handed it back, it simply said, "Take the latter!" I know I had a look of dismay on my face, because down deep I wanted to join the force. He was so intent that I shouldn't. My look of disappointment was no doubt quite obvious. He again wrote something, "Remember what I told you!" I shook my head in the affirmative, all the while staring down at the floor. Web tapped the pen on the table, and I looked up at him. There seemed to be a look of empathy, and understanding on his face. Again he wrote something for me. He turned the pad so I could read it. It caught me by surprise!

"Have you and Lily got any wedding plans?"

Not only did his question surprise me, it put me in a much better mood. I wrote my answer; "Most definitely!" He took the pad and wrote what was another surprise! "I have some wedding gifts for you."

Wow! That's great I thought. I couldn't wait to tell Lily. I wrote that on the writing pad and added, "Any hints?"

Web read it, hesitated then wrote; "If you give people hints, they might figure it out and then it wouldn't be a surprise!"

I chuckled because I was never good with figuring things out, and wrote that back to him. Then I took back the pad and added, "Come on, give me a shot."

Web grinned, as he slowly reached for the pad. He wrote something, and then stopped, not lifting the pen from the paper. It was a like a few moments in suspended animation. Finally he wrote a little more and handed it to me. My first reaction was, what the hell is this? What does he mean? He had written, "The Three Jimmies." The only answer I could come up with, that would likely make me appear in left field, where I did spend a lot time. I wrote, "3 SUV's?" Web had a good silent laugh and then shook his head no, taking the sheet he had written on, crumpled it up and threw it in the garbage can. He pointed to his watch, same old message, school time. I wrote him one more word, "Later?" He nodded in the affirmative, and off I went.

After school I noticed Web's pick-up was gone, so I went to pick up Lily. My very first words were predictable to say the least. She was very smart, and I knew she would probably have the answer in no time. I asked her what she thought "The Three Jimmies" meant. She looked at me kind of strange, and I gathered she might think me slow, for not knowing the answer. Her answer was not what I expected, she said, "I haven't got the foggiest". Great, now what? Then I told her that this was what Web called a wedding gift for us. Lily thought for a moment, then said, "Maybe it's a place? Wait. I've got an idea. Why don't you come over to my house and I'll check it out on the Net?"

"The Internet?" I asked in doubting fashion, since I had very little interest in anything to do with computers.

"Well sure, why not? You can find just about anything on the Net!"

Reluctantly I agreed, and off we were to find a website to find out what "The Three Jimmies" might be.

Our trip to Lily's house and use her computer wasn't going to work. When we got there her younger brother was busy on the computer completing a school project. Not to be foiled, Lily suggested we go back to my school library and use one of those computers. Off we went and when we arrived at the library and she did her thing.

Lily flew through all kinds of sites to find anything that would link up to "The Three Jimmies." Nothing. Another five minutes. Nothing. Another ten minutes, still nothing. Time to give up I told her.

"I can't find anything. Any other ideas?"

"No, not me. I was sure it had to do with SUV's but Web said no."

"Well I don't know where else to look. It has nothing to do with news stories, places, or anything as far as I can tell. It's got to mean something else."

"That's okay, you tried. I'll ask him again tomorrow for another hint. Let's let it go for now."

Well, the final day of school finally arrived. What a relief it had finally come. Aside from some of the bigger issues I was facing, I was focused on finding Web and asking him for more details about "The Three Jimmies."

As I drove into the school parking lot, I couldn't help but notice an odd sight. There at the front entrance were three identical black Chevy Tahoes. Impressive I thought, but odd in the sense that they looked very "Official." I wondered what was going on, but sure that I'd find out in short order. First I wanted to find Web. When I rang the bell for office, there was no response. I tried the door, but it was locked. I looked all around for his pick-up, but it was nowhere in sight. I figured I'd catch up to him later, so I went in the school for my very last time.

Making my way to class I saw a group of men in dark suits coming out of the principal's office. I chuckled to myself, these guys look like they're right out of some movie involving Federal Agents. I asked a couple of kids what was going on and they said they didn't know. I walked down the hallway and went to my class. I leaned over to talk to Sandra, and asked her if she knew what was going on. She shrugged her shoulders and said, "I don't know for sure, but I heard those men came in the school, went right into the library for a time, and then went into the principal's office."

By the time she finished her sentence, a cold chill had run down my spine. Could this have something to do with Lily and I searching the Net last night? My mind raced on full speed thinking the worst. I regained my composure. Who was I kidding? I must be watching too many movies. The chances that simply searching the Net had anything to do with today's events was likely so remote, maybe I should just give my head a shake!

That wasn't working. I started worrying about Lily and Web! I asked the teacher to be excused. I got attitude in return, so I just told him too bad, I had more important things to attend to. I raced out of the school and checked to see if Web's truck was there, it wasn't. I ran to his office, and the door was still locked. Next, I had to get to Lily's school. I slowed down, fearing that I might be drawing undue attention to myself. Driving out of the parking lot I saw the Black Tahoes were still parked out front. On my way to Lily's school I went by Web's house and again no pick-up in the yard, no sign of Web. I sped past his place and over to see Lily. I ran into the school, to the room where her first class was. I knocked on the door and her teacher answered. I told her I needed to talk to Lily right away, it was urgent. Her response so typified many a teacher. She gave me the "Look here sonny" expression, and tried to tell me how irregular this was. With a firm angry tone, and a pounding of my fist on the wall, I told her I was going in to get her. She snapped back immediately with the

"Principal" threat, but then acknowledged that Lily never showed up for class that morning.

I charged out of the school and got in my car. I had to get over to Lily's house. With no respect for the speed limit, I made it to her house in less than four minutes. I slammed the brakes on in front of her house. My heart was just a pounding, fearing something was wrong. I ran up to the door, banged on it with my fist, but no answer. I kept banging, still no answer. Just as I went back to my car, I heard Lily. She called down to me from the bedroom window. I took a moment to catch my breath.

"What's all the banging about?" she asked.

"Oh man, am I glad to see you!"

"What's going on?"

"Look, can you come down so I can talk to you?"

A few minutes later she came down to the car. She looked very worried and again asked what was wrong.

"I just wanted to be sure your okay and safe."

"Quint, don't slough me off like that. It's not going to work. What's going on?"

"How come you weren't at school?"

"Quint, tell me what's up!"

I told Lily what was going on at my school and that I didn't know where Web was. Lily had a calming effect in many situations, and this was one of them. She got me to think things through. First of all, she had slept in that was why she wasn't at school. As far as Web, he could have been out on school business, something he needed, or whatever. I realized that I had got all stressed and worried for nothing, and had worried her for nothing. I felt a sense of relief, and relaxation, having her help me put things in perspective. I drove her to her school, and told her I'd pick her up at lunch.

On my way back to my school, I decided to have one more

look for Web. I stopped at his house. No pick-up, no Web. I went over to the garage to see if his truck was in there. The side door was locked, same as the main door, so I looked in the window. There was a vehicle in the garage but it wasn't a truck, it was a car. Well, the only thing left to do was go back to the school and hope he's there.

Heading back to the school, I felt very frustrated over the morning's events. I took O'Brien Street, and came to the four-way stop. Just as I was ready to turn right, I noticed in my mirror a blue pick-up coming flashing his headlights. It was Web. He came racing up beside me, and yells out, "Follow me!" He took off in the opposite direction, so I swung around to follow him and caught up to him in a few seconds. Then it hit me! He can speak!

He turned onto a side street and pulled over. I came up beside him. He got out and climbed into my car. Web could see the shocked look on my face. He simply said, "Okay kid, just drive." I was lost for words! What was happening here? I couldn't believe this!

"Head down to Foster Street and hang a right."

I followed his instructions. But to say the least, I deserved an explanation!

"Okay, so you can speak, that's great! Now, how about some kind of explanation of what the hell this is all about?"

"Well, I guess I really don't have much choice now. First thing, rest assured I am your friend. I'm not out to hurt you or cause you any pain. I quite simply never should have thrown 'The Three Jimmies' at you."

"You mean all this has something to do with 'The Three Jimmies'?"

"I'm afraid so."

"So is that what those guys were at the school about this morning?"

"Absolutely, and I gather you used a library computer to search for, 'The Three Jimmies'?"

"Well, yeah, we did. How was I supposed to know this would happen?"

"Hey, I shouldn't have said anything. I'm sorry I got you involved in this!"

"Involved in what?"

"Nothing, actually. The Feds don't know it was you that was searching for the 'The Three Jimmies.'"

"So those were Federal Agents at the school?"

"Yeah, I'm afraid they were. See up ahead there; pull in behind the coffee shop."

Chapter Four

Each day we face many challenges; some large, some small. Each day we deal with them as best we can. Then every once in a while, a challenge exceeds what we may view large, and could be classed as seemingly insurmountable.

This was exactly what my day's events were shaping up to. I pulled in behind the coffee shop as Web had told me, wondering how I would deal with all this, and all that I would still need to be enlightened on? I stopped the car, and looked over at Web. "Okay, now what?"

"Listen, I know you've got a lot of questions you want answered. Just bear with me for a few minutes. I've got to use the pay phone, so why don't you go in and get us a couple of coffees."

"Whatever." I replied as I grabbed my keys from the ignition, all the while watching Web. He walked over to the phone, noticing he didn't put any change in it. I was sure he pushed zero for the operator. Web turned and looked back at the car and motioned for me to go in and get the coffees. Reluctantly I went in to do so. Somehow I sensed that today had some more surprises in store for me.

I got back to the car as quick as I could. Web was just coming out of the phone booth. He got in the car and I handed him his coffee. Without saying a word he lifted the lid and took a sip.

"Shit! Man, why can't any of these places make a decent cup of coffee? This tastes like crap. I wonder what their secret is?"

"I can't believe you, after everything that's happened today, you're hung up on coffee?"

"Quint, you know getting all stressed and upset isn't going to change what's going on."

"Pray do tell. What is going on?"

He stared out the window for a few seconds. Then rubbed his beard, and scratched at it. "I hate this damn beard!"

"Well then shave if off!" I snapped back, frustrated at not getting any answers.

"I can't do that. It's part of how I stay in hiding."

"Hiding from what?" I asked raising my voice.

"What do think! The Feds, isn't it obvious?"

"What on earth did you do that put the Feds onto you?"

For anyone to have Federal Agents looking for them, would seem to be painting a picture that was very dark, with no light present. A flurry of thoughts flooded my mind wondering who Web really was. Was he a mass murderer, or some kind of psycho? I needed to get some understanding of who or what I was becoming a part of. So I repeated my question. "Please tell me what the hell is going on?" I was pleading with him, pleading for an answer.

"I owe you that much kid." He took another slow sip of his coffee. The suspense was driving me crazy, yet through all of this he didn't seem frazzled at all. Finally he opened up.

"The first thing I want you to know is that I'm not a murderer, I'm not a thief, nor am I a liar. What you need to know, is that the less you know about me the safer it is for you. What I'm involved in, or should say was involved in was a long time ago, and I cut all ties with these people. I want nothing to do with them. What I did in the past was under orders. I was just doing my job."

Sarcastically I asked, "Which was?"

"Look, I just told you, the less you know the safer it is."

"What are the Feds going to do, shoot me on sight for hanging around with you?"

He looked at me with that cold piercing look, and suddenly I realized this was far more serious than I was taking it. He didn't answer my question, yet without uttering a word, I felt an ice cold answer had been given, in the affirmative. The moment of silence continued.

It would seem what I was viewing as a challenge was all that and more. What would be my next move? How was I to deal with this, especially when he had told me so little?

It was a sobering thought indeed that these people after Web wouldn't hesitate to "shoot to kill." At this point I realized it was more than mere curiosity that I was experiencing. I had grown fond of Web, and now that his life was in danger, there must be something I could do to help. When I asked him, he reacted with a dubious look, as if he doubted any notion that I could help.

"You have no idea what's going on, or who you would be up against if you became involved. The best way to help is stay out of the picture." I was about to speak up, when he put up his opened hand and said, "I know. I know you want to do something, but trust me. Everything will work out. In a few hours the Feds will have done their thing, and they'll be gone. Then things will get back to normal."

"Sounds like wishful thinking."

Web didn't respond. He re-focused on his coffee. I wasn't about to give in this easy.

"So, what's the plan?" He looked at his watch, and said, "Give me about five minutes."

Those next five minutes were very quiet. I figured that he wanted not only his space but some quiet time to think things out. On top of that, I was sure he was expecting a call. Sure enough the pay phone rang and he got out to answer. I watched as his conversation went from calm to quite animated! He looked very upset. He had been so calm, but this was different. He slammed the receiver on the window then hung up the phone. He hustled back to the car. "Okay, kid, let's roll."

"Where to?"

"Take me my place."

"Your house? They'll be watching your place. Why there?"

"I know what I'm doing just move it!" Then he said something under his breath, but I caught it. He said the house wasn't in his name.

As we got close he said, "Don't take my street, let me off at the house behind mine. I've got something I have to get out of the garage. You be on your way I'll be fine."

"No way!" I shouted. "I can't just take off and leave you!"

"Yes, you have to. By now, they'll have their sights fixed on me because I'm probably the only personnel from the school that's not accounted for. Secondly, by now they'll know you had a connection to me, and they'll be looking for you via your car. This blue and white Chevelle is not very inconspicuous."

I knew all too well that he had a valid point. I watched him walk toward his garage. All was quiet for a few minutes. I certainly didn't want to be the link that enabled the Feds to nail him. I struggled with my limited options, then I heard it. I wasn't sure where it was coming from. I got out of my car, the sound was an unmistakable one. A unique sound that could only be one thing. The noise came from the other street right by Web's garage. I had to drive over. There it was! It was backing out of Web's driveway and he was in it! I couldn't believe my eyes! Web was driving one of North America's most prized machines; a 1969 Yellow Yenko Camaro! I forgot about everything else and drove up beside him. He instantly started shaking his head at me.

"Quint, get out of here now." I knew he was right, but I wanted another option.

"Look, can I follow you at a distance?"

"No. No way! Just boot it on out of here!"

"No, I'm going to keep my distance and follow you. And don't speed 'cause that will draw attention to you."

He rested his head on the steering wheel. I knew he was exasperated. But my persistence paid off.

"Do you know that old back road, Sterling Side Road?"

Excitedly I answered, "Yes!"

"Give me a twenty minute head start. You go and duck in behind the coffee shop 'til then. Make sure to take Mason Avenue and then the lane way to Sterling. There shouldn't be any Feds around there."

"Where will you be on Sterling?"

"Take Sterling for about seven miles. Watch for me on the left. Now get!"

The next twenty minutes seemed like hours. At last I was on my way. To where? I wasn't sure. I followed his directions and came near the seven mile spot on Sterling. There was no sign of Web or his car. I slowed down, looking for any sign. Then all of a sudden someone stepped out from the brush, it was Web!

"I wish you would follow all the instructions I give you, the same as you did these." He didn't look too impressed.

"Where's your car?"

"Just pull up ahead, there's a narrow driveway." Sure enough, well hidden by trees and brush, was a narrow driveway. His car was parked by a gate. He told me to follow him through and then he would lock the gate. As we drove the rest of the driveway, very narrow to say the least, we came to a clearing. There nestled among the tall pines was a beautiful log cabin. Behind it was Parson's Lake. The setting was breathtaking. I wished Lily could be here to see this. I expressed my thoughts as, "Awesome!"

Web smiled and walked up onto the porch, sitting down on one of the arm chairs.

"You might as well come up here and have a seat."

It felt good to be here, and be invited to sit with him. When I sat down he asked, "Do you want a drink?"

"Sure!" I lightened right up thinking I could use a good drink. He went in the cabin and came out with two tall glasses with, of all things, water! He saw my reaction and asked, "What did you think I meant?" I just grinned, took the glass and had a drink. Realizing that answers to my questions had been few and far between, I thought of a different approach.

"I've got to hand it to you, that was an ingenious disguising of yourself with the deaf mute act. You sure had me fooled!"

He shrugged it off with, "Just part of my survival routine."

After he said it, it hit me. Part of surviving would include a new identity. "So I guess that William E. Brown is merely your new or latest name. Oh yes, I know! You can't tell me your real name." There was an obvious tone of sarcasm, which I shouldn't have done. Web remained quiet. I thought of a way to diffuse my insult. "William E. Brown, was a pretty good choice, seeing that there's probably a few thousand people named that in the States."

"Actually, well over ten thousand."

I had a good laugh. "That'll keep the Feds busy!"

"That's the plan."

"So, can I ask what your real name is?"

His expression softened. I was surprised. I had expected a harsher reaction.

"My real name—that's long gone. You call me Web, that's the name you know me by."

He then changed the subject. "Look, I'm going to be staying here for a few days until the dust settles. It'll be dark in a couple of hours. Then you can head back to town, but go the long way. Take Sterling Side Road to the north end, and then get back to town on Highway Thirty-Five. And one more thing."

His next comment caught me off guard.

"Can I trust you?"

"Yes. Yes of course. Definitely!"

"No word about me, this place, everything about today, to no one. Not even Lily."

"Well, Lily knows about the Feds, because I went looking for her after they showed up, and I told her they were at the school."

"Okay. Don't say anymore to her, and do not talk to her on the phone or your cell phone."

"Why?"

"Because they've manipulated the phone system."

"What?"

"Yeah. Just do as I ask. Don't give them an inch, 'cause they'll take more than a mile."

I reasoned if he felt he could trust me would he let me know more?

"Since I've assured you I won't talk to anyone about all this, can you tell me at least why these guys are after you?"

"You know kid, it's human nature to be curious. But what you know is already more than you should."

"But I understand that what you did was following orders. I believe that! Why can't you elaborate?"

He looked frustrated. He closed his eyes and put his head in his hands. Then he sat up. He held his two opened hands out in front of me.

"Okay. It's like this. What do you see here?"

"Two hands?" I couldn't see where this was going.

"How would you describe them?"

"Gee, uh, left and right?"

"That's correct. Now think of the Government, think of it like this." Still with both hands opened in front of me, "The Government has a Right and a Left hand. It's known exclusively for its Right hand. I worked for the Left hand, taking care of business that the Right hand knew virtually nothing about. We looked after matters in the country in ways the Right hand never could. There would never be any serious repercussions for the Right, because the Left is virtually unknown, and undetectable. The Left stayed hidden behind the scenes."

"Interesting concept." My response was a line I was told once to use when you don't fully understand something complicated. I didn't want to look stupid, but it was too late. Web could tell I didn't really get the picture. He gave one of those half smiles and said no more. Then I realized there was another angle here to approach him with.

"So, 'The Three Jimmies' has to do with a Left handed, should I call it, 'Assignment'?"

"Yeah." He raised his eyebrows, with that don't ask anymore questions look.

I was cautious about pressing him too far. Most of what he shared with me was more like a riddle. Riddles, something I was never good at figuring out. I decided to change the subject, to his car.

"Where did you ever find that beauty?"

"Came across her in Arizona, back about twenty years ago. Some guy needed the money and I happened to be there at the right time. He was driving through the desert, from town to town looking for work. Flat broke. And I've been caring for the old girl ever sinc –."

He stopped and changed gears rather unexpectedly, "Be sure to let me know when you and Lily set your wedding date!"

"Absolutely. You'll be the first to know." I wanted to bring up 'The Three Jimmies,' but I knew it wasn't the right time.

"Now remember, when you get to town the Feds are going to want to talk to you. Just play dumb. Ignorance does have its place. For sure they've talked to Lily and they'll want you to help put the pieces of their puzzle together."

I didn't like the idea of having to lie, but it would be the only way to protect Web. Then I felt a sense of panic. "What about this cabin. It's just a matter of time before they trace it to you! Even as common as the name William Brown is."

"Relax. William E. Brown doesn't own this cabin. And he doesn't own the car, or the house in town. You don't need to know the other names, but rest assured, after years of hiding, I try to keep all loose ends well tied. The Feds are on a wild goose chase looking for William E. Brown. All there going to find is a savings account at First National, with about fifty bucks in it. If they view the Surveillance tapes, all they'll see is some old guy, with a hat, and a full beard cashing his paycheck, who never said a word to a teller in all the years he banked there."

A true sense of relief came over me. But the one name I wanted to know so much, would be the one he guarded the most. But I had to try again. "Of all those names you have, why won't you tell me the real one?"

"That name is gone. I told you that."

"How about just your first name?"

"Give it up did. End of conversation. You get ready to head back."

Chapter Five

Web remained seated on the porch. The sound of the wind as it swept through the pine trees was like a whispering sound. How I wished it would whisper some of Web's secrets. I pondered the day's events. My mind was flooded with so many questions. I worried that he might not remain here as he said he would. Was this his way of getting me out of the picture? Was he about to disappear? The only way to know for sure would be to leave and come back a short time later. He got up from his seat on the porch.

"Don't forget to lock the gate when you leave."

"No problem."

In an effort to conceal the fact that I was coming back I asked him, "How can I get a hold of you to make sure your okay?"

"I'll be okay." That moment he turned sharply to side and it looked like he grabbed his chest. He took a deep breath and turned around. He was in pain. He often squinted when he looked at me with his piercing look, but this was more intense. His look had pain written all over it. Before I could say a word, he said, "Better be on your way."

"Are you feeling okay?"

"Damn it! I'm fine!" He paused for a moment. Then said: "One more thing!" This time his look was the usual piercing, squinting look. He had read my mind. "Don't even think about coming back here later, or tomorrow, or the next day. You got that?"

He held out his hand to shake mine. As we shook, I felt there was a sense of finality in his look. He looked me straight in the eye. The sense of finality was that this might be the last time I see him. Something wasn't right with this picture. His handshake was weak. Not like before. It was disturbing. Stepping off the porch, walking toward my car, I thought of some way to convince him to let me stay. If I didn't persevere now, I might never know the truth of what's happening, and may never see him again. I stopped, turned around, and said, "You've got to tell me more!" I took two steps toward him and stopped. Our eyes locked. He stood still on the porch giving with me that penetrating look. Not a word was spoken. The silence of the moment was deafening. The seconds ticked so slowly. My mind went blank as to what to say next. Web saved me the trouble. To my complete surprise he told me to come in the cabin. I was ecstatic! Would this be the first step to some answers?

Walking into the cabin was like walking into a picture in a magazine. It was so inviting, so calming, with its huge stone fireplace, and large windows giving a great view of the lake. I knew that this is what I wanted for Lily and I some day. Web told me to have a seat on the couch. He paced back and forth in front of the fireplace.

He looked like someone with lots on his mind but wasn't sharing it. He was definitely troubled. He put a CD in the stereo, and sat in the arm chair. As the music began to play, he leaned his head back, closed his eyes, likely to absorb the music's peaceful effect. The song that played was "Air" by Bach. Web appeared totally relaxed. I remained silent as the piece played. When it finished he looked at me and said, "Sometimes you just have to stop and breathe the 'Air', know what I mean? Certain music helps me relax, and collect my thoughts. You should try it."

Obviously I didn't look relaxed. He made a suggestion. "Maybe I should put that on again, and you lean back, close your eyes, and breathe the 'Air.'" I obliged, and it did have a calming effect. His next words showed his appreciation for such classical works.

"Beautiful music like this will always have a selection of stringed instruments, especially the Violas, which should be at the center of every orchestra."

When the piece finished its second spin, Web made a promise. "When the time is right, I'll tell you more. But you've got to remember that being in hiding, means just that, hiding.

The less people know the better chance of staying hidden. For now, I'm going to lay low."

It was more of the same, and I was getting frustrated all over again. It was as if he was spinning a web and keeping me trapped in the dark. He still hadn't told me anything.

"Hey kid, don't look so dejected. You have to understand I've stayed hidden for almost twenty-five years. I know what I'm doing. You don't like the way I approach the matter, but I don't have many options. Please understand. I keep you at arms length to protect you. Now, before you go, have you got three bucks on you?"

"Three bucks? What's that got to do with all of this?"

"It's for a good cause. Trust me."

I gave him the money, and he added, "You'll know more soon enough!"

It was no use entertaining any thought of an explanation. I knew it would be in vain. I would have to trust him. I got into my car, glanced at him one last time, and he gave me the thumbs up signal. I left. But I was going to do one thing my way. I drove down Sterling Side Road until I got to Highway Thirty-Five, and drove in the other direction. I stopped at a diner, took a window seat and ordered a meal. I was going to take my time and sit here to see if he goes by. I was there quite awhile, but no sign of Web. I started driving back around ten o'clock, but still didn't feel right about this. I drove back down Sterling Side Road to within half-a-mile of Web's cabin. I was going to sit right there until morning. If he was going to leave, I would know it. I left my window down a bit and settled in for the night.

The morning sun was refreshing, but that was going to be the limit for anything refreshing as far as this day was concerned. Since there was no sign of Web on the move, it was time to check on Lily.

Traveling back to town on the route Web gave me, my focus was mostly on Lily. I was worried about her, but couldn't call her. Strange I thought, there was nothing on my phone to show that she tried to get a hold of me. I planned to go to her house as soon as I got back to town.

It took about half an hour to get back to town by way of Highway Thirty-Five. As I drove past the town sign "Welcome to Masonville", there they were, parked just behind the sign, a black Tahoe. As soon as I went by they pulled out onto the highway. Watching them in my rear view mirror, they stayed back a fair distance, just like the movies. But trying to stay calm about all this, I sure wasn't kidding myself. This was reality. My heart was pounding. These guys were for real! Still, as best I could, I'd have to act like nothing was wrong or different in any way. I continued on to Lily's house. That was most important!

No sooner had I pulled into her driveway, when the Feds pulled up right in front of the house. Nonchalantly I went up to her door, pretending to be unaware of their presence. I knocked but no answer. Same thing the second time I tried. I turned to go to the back door, when I was confronted by two men, completely obvious with their dark suits, and of course, shades! The taller one asked, "Are you Quint Matthews?"

"Yeah, who are you guys, the Mod Squad?" My lame effort at a joke did not go over well. In terse fashion he said, "FBI", then showed me his I.D., as did his partner.

"I'm Agent Wallace, and this is Agent Phillips., we'd like to ask you a few questions."

In my continued effort to make light of the situation, I said "Can I see those badges again?" Wallace looked at Phillips, frowned, then took out his I.D. He held it out in front of my face, and I looked at it up close, squinting, pretending to study it very carefully. Neither he nor his sidekick look impressed, as was clear with his next remark.

"You know kid, we don't need your permission to ask you questions, so cut the crap, and this charade!" I sat down on Lily's front step and replied, "Okay, so you guys must be for real, what's going on?"

"We understand you're acquainted with a William E. Brown?" Phillips asked.

Endeavoring to appear unaffected by the question, I answered, "Yeah, he's the old guy who looks after the high school grounds."

"Do you know where he is?" asked Philips.

My response was presented very sarcastically. "How should I know? Did you check the school?"

That evoked an immediate retort from Wallace, "Look, kid, don't play games with us. This is serious! We can have you charged with hindering a Federal Investigation!"

"I'm not trying to hinder anything. How should I know where he is, I'm not his keeper, he's a loner!"

It was becoming apparent they weren't taking this lightly!

Wallace piped up, "This is your last chance. Once more. Do you know where he is?"

It troubled me to lie, but I wouldn't give up Web. I made

certain to look Wallace straight in the eye with my answer, fully aware of the methodology in detecting eye movement, and the like, in determining truthful statements or false. In a very emphatic tone told him, "I don't know."

Wallace maintained eye contact with me, obviously watching my eye movement. To change direction I asked, "What did he do? Rob some armored car?"

To my surprise, Philips answered with, "A lot worse than that. If you know where he is, you already know too much. You're a marked man if you do."

I shrugged my shoulders, hoping my lack of emotion, or reaction, would take them off the scent.

He reached inside his jacket pocket, and for a second I thought he was reaching for his gun. Instead he pulled out some photos and said, "Here's what happened to some people that got too close to Mr. Brown."

The pictures were gruesome. As I went through them, I felt sick. I stopped looking at the stack, cautious not to give anything away by my reaction. All through this, Wallace had continued his intent glare.

"Okay. So the guy's a murderer. If I see him, I'll call the police right away!"

I handed the stack of photos back to Philips. Wallace wouldn't quit glaring at me. His hostility was quite evident now. Perhaps in an effort to portray the "Good cop, bad cop" routine, Philips in a very soft, kind tone said, "One of the people in the photos was about your age, son. You don't realize what you've gotten into here. This Brown character shows no remorse, no concern whatsoever for human life."

Still I was determined not to give Web up. I reasoned that they could show me any pictures and tell me what ever they wanted. However I was caught off guard by Philips next comment.

"You have a girlfriend named Lily?" My reaction proved my inexperience in these fields. I nervously stuttered twice then asked, "Why are you bringing up Lily?"

Philips answered with, "Why don't you take a look at the last picture in the stack."

Reluctantly I took a look. "Oh God!" was all I could answer. I shoved the stack back in his hand. I couldn't get the picture of the murdered girl out of my head. But then Philips told me more. "This was the girlfriend of the young man about your age that Mr. Brown also murdered."

A dead silence set in. I wasn't kidding anyone at this point. They knew they had got to me. The charade was over. For the first time through all of this, my sense of loyalty to Web was shaken. Philip's next question was about to put a crack in that loyalty.

"Do you know where your girlfriend is right now?"

A cold shiver made its way down my spine. Both of them could tell by the look on my face, the look of fear and uncertainty that they had got to me. Wallace had a triumphant look about him, the self satisfied creep, and Philips looked very pleased with himself.

I pointed to the front door, and knew my voice was getting shaky. "Lily's not home."

"We know. We've already been here!" Wallace had a smile, of all things, on his face.

This whole episode wasn't sitting well. I contemplated what further response would be fitting. I knew in my heart, there's no way Web would ever hurt Lily! These Feds were trying to push some buttons with me. They probably had Lily down at the police station. I recalled Web's advice, "Ignorance has its place." I thought of something else he told me. All that he did, he was following orders, and that he was no murderer. I was going to stick to my guns.

With renewed confidence I took a deep breath and told them, "I can't help you guys, I just don't know where he is and that's not a Federal offence."

Neither one of them said anything. I walked over to my car, and I'm sure they never took their eyes off me. I started my car, and knew of course they would follow. Let's make this a little more interesting. I lit up the old girl, depositing excessive amounts of rubber on the pavement. Sure enough the two Stooges came barreling after me. Little did they know I was headed for the police station. I was sure Lily was there. When I got there, well ahead of the Stooges, I went in and asked for the Sheriff. Apparently he wasn't in. I looked around while the deputy went to answer the phone. Down the hallway were four rooms, all the doors were shut. Determined to find her I tried every door. The first room was empty, same as the second. I could hear some voices in the third room. I knew those voices. Another cold chill found its way down my spine. Those voices were Lily parents; Mr. and Mrs. Parker. Lily must be in there with them.

I flung the door open, and stopped cold. No Lily! My heart sank. Mr. Parker had his arm around his wife's shoulder. They both had their heads down. Mrs. Parker was crying. They looked up at me with such a look of despair. Something was terribly wrong. A sinking feeling came over me.

"Where's Lily?" I yelled.

"Are you Quint, the boyfriend?" One of the Agents in the dark suit sitting across from the Parkers asked me.

I snapped back, "I'm not talking to you!"

Mrs. Parker pleaded, "Oh Quint! Have you seen Lily?"

"I dropped her off at school this morning."

The same Agent spoke up, "Well, she didn't show up at school. So you're the last person to see her."

My mind raced with possible scenarios. But wait, Web

couldn't have hurt Lily. After I dropped her off at school, I went looking for him. He come racing up behind me in his pick-up, and I was with him almost all of the day until I came back to town. He had asked about our wedding and the date. He couldn't have anything do this with this. Then it hit me! Yes, it had to be.

I looked at the two Agents sitting in the room. In a very deliberate, strong tone, I said to them, "YOU GUYS!" Pointing my finger at them, and again saying, "YOU GUYS! You have her! You're using her to get to me!"

Mr. Parker jumped to his feet and yelled, "What the hell is going on here? I demand to know!"

At that point, Agents Wallace and Philips came into the room. Wallace was obviously in charge as he looked at the other two Agents, and shook his head ever so slightly as to say "No." Wallace didn't want the other Agents to respond to the question. Mr. Parker repeated his question, and demanded an explanation.

To say I was extremely suspicious of these Agents would be an understatement. It was evident they would go to great lengths to snag Web. Now they were using Lily as bait. I had to keep a cool head. I asked myself, what would Web do right now? I remembered the plaque in his office, "A time to speak and a time to be quiet." Best thing I could do right now was to stand back, listen, and survey the situation.

Mr. Parker again put his arm around his wife, trying to comfort her. This was a painful ordeal for them. All was silent for the moment, until Sheriff Wilson came into the room.

"Good day folks. I know how worried you must be!" His down to earth approach brought some improvement to the tense atmosphere in the room. "I want to assure you folks that all of us in this room are concerned for Lily. But we have all got to work together, and give a hundred percent co-operation." He then looked directly at me, "That includes you too, Quint. I want you to show respect for all the badges in this room!"

As he finished speaking I realized this was an interrogation room, which meant the mirror on the end wall had to be a two way mirror. Sheriff Wilson must have been on the other side of the mirror, and that was the only room I hadn't checked! The question of course, who was in there with him? My "Time to be quiet" had passed.

"Who's on the other side of the glass, Sheriff?"

"Now, Quint—" Before he could finish, Wallace interrupted.

"The Sheriff just told you to show some respect for all the badges in this room! That means we ask the questions, and you concern yourself with only answers."

I looked at the mirror. I fixed my stare, wishing it could be as penetrating as Web's. Sheriff Wilson went over to the corner of the room and stood there quietly. Mrs. Parker began to weep again. Agent Philips reassured the Parkers that the FBI was here to help, then employing a new tactic, asked them to convince me to co-operate. A true "Back door" maneuver, but it was effective. Mr. Parker immediately reacted.

"Please Quint, please, if you know anything about this, please tell them. Help us find Lily!" I assured him I didn't know where she was. By now I was more than incensed at these Agents. I was sure they were behind this. I pointed my finger at Wallace, and in a firm tone said, "HE KNOWS! AND SO DOES HE!" Pointing to Agent Philips. "AND SO DOES HE!" I shouted pointing at the mirror.

Mrs. Parker sobbed ever so loudly, and Mr. Parker stood up, and in a rage threw his chair against the wall. "Someone in here is lying! If my daughter is hurt because of one of you I'll kill you with my bare hands!"

Wallace gestured gently to Mr. Parker, and said, "Everyone just take a moment to catch their breath. Just sit tight, I'll be right back. Sheriff would you please get these folks some coffee?"

Wallace turned to leave and cast a disgusted look my way, which he made sure I saw.

Silence descended upon the room for a second time. As it did, my inner fears and turmoil kept mounting. I was so worried about what Lily might be going through at the hands of the Feds! These Agents, these guys were bad news. How could they take her and use her this way? Suddenly I realized, wait, could she be in the next room on the other side of the mirror? Was this part of some sick mind game they were orchestrating? Slowly I moved toward the door, quickly grabbed the knob, opened it and rushed into the hallway to the next room. I opened the door but it only opened about halfway, so I put my weight against and shoved hard! I hadn't realized Wallace was in the way and when I shoved hard against the door it sat him on his ass. A loud thud confirmed it, as my two hundred and twenty pounds were no match for his mere a hundred and sixty pounds. I stood in the opened doorway, seeing him on the floor. As he stood up, he reached in his jacket and pulled out his gun.

"That's it Matthews! You're under arrest. You just assaulted a Federal Agent! I'm not taking any more crap from you!"

As he took out his hand cuffs, a low voice came out of the shadows.

"It's all right, let him alone."

The room was fairly dark, so I couldn't make out a face, but could tell someone was standing off to the side. I looked around the room for Lily, but no Lily! There was no one else in the room. Wallace was ticked, and still stood beside me with the cuffs in his hand. The same low voice told him, "Just let him go."

"Who are you?" I asked.

"Special Agent Hastings." He stepped forward out of the shadows. He looked quite distinguished, not your typical FBI stereotypes like Wallace and Philips. There was a distinct calmness about him. He stood there with his hands behind his back, smiling at me. Was this another case of "Good cop, bad cop?" I wasn't sure, but his calming effect continued, as he spoke to me.

"You're free to go son. All we ask is that you be available if we need to talk to you. I do want to emphasize, that we are concerned for your safety, and your girlfriend's as well. Please be assured we are trying to find her. And I must warn you that Mr. William E. Brown is, without a doubt, a very dangerous man." He still hadn't broke eye contact with me.

I turned to leave, but apparently Hastings wasn't finished yet.

"Before you go, there is something else. I understand the name you use for Mr. Brown, is Web?"

"Yeah, that's what I call him."

"So, when you call him Web, can he hear you?"

It was obvious he wasn't buying Web's disguise. I opted not to answer. Hastings still had his hands behind his back, but now looked up at the ceiling, as he spoke.

"Interesting name you have for Mr. Brown. You know when I think of the name, or word, 'Web', I think of entanglement. Something a person might get himself into and have an extremely hard time getting out of. I hope that's not the case with you Son."

Again I didn't respond. Perhaps I should have. But he had still more to say. Looking at me straight in the eye, he finished his little speech.

"On a final note, just so you know what to expect from me from here on in. It's much the same as what they say in that song. I'm sure you know it. "Every breath you take, every move you make, every step you take, I'll be watching you!"

Chapter Six

Leaving the police station I was haunted by question after question pouring through my mind. Was I making a mistake not to co-operate? Was I jeopardizing Lily's safety? What about Web's safety? I knew that if I co-operated with the Feds, I'd be turning Web in. I was struggling with the fact that some seeds of doubt were taking root. The only way to think clearly would be to get back to Web! Even though he wants me to stay away, I need to talk to him. I need some re-assurance from him.

Getting into my car, I knew they would be watching my every move. So for me to get back to Web, I'd have to come up with some way to elude Hastings and his buddies. The main problem is that they're watching all the roads in and out of town. I thought of switching vehicles. However, that wouldn't work, because they would be checking out the drivers. My options had dwindled quickly, and I was down to what was likely my only option. I stopped at the Delmar Diner to grab a bite and think this through.

My last and only option became clear. Water! Parsons Creek that wound its way through town and ran to Parsons Lake would lead to where Web's cabin is. This still left me with at least two problems. Number one, how to get a canoe to the creek, and number two, I hate the water! For now, I'd have to go back to my apartment and figure some way to make this work. I'd have to wait for dark anyway, and that was at least five hours away.

One of the problems was a canoe. I thought of Lenny Baxter,

he had one. But I realized my phone was tapped, and even if I use a pay phone, Web had said they've manipulated the phone system. I had to think of another way to get a canoe.

I walked up the stairs to my apartment and unlocked the door. I saw that my answering machine was indicating one message. Before I could push the play button, I heard a voice, "Don't bother, we already checked it. You have a movie rental that's two days late."

There they were sitting in my apartment; Agents Wallace and Agents Philips. After my initial shock, I expressed my disgust. "What the hell gives you the right to break into my apartment?" In typical fashion Wallace show me his FBI Badge, and said, "We can do anything we want kid. This badge gives us the right."

"The right? The right my ass! Get the hell out of here! I've got nothing to say!"

"What are you going to do, pull a Boo Radley on us?" Wallace replied with his usual sarcasm. I wondered what he was talking about. Philips could tell by my puzzled look that I didn't get it. So he said, "You know, the dummy in *To Kill a Mockingbird*." I thought for a moment, and yes, I got the point. He was the silent character. I decided to return the sarcasm.

"I might be a Boo Radley, but you're no Atticus Finch. You're not intelligent enough."

Our exchange of insults ended there, for no sooner had I finished speaking, Wallace looked over to the doorway. I turned to see Special Agent Hastings standing there, hands behind his back, smiling. Once again, he had a calming effect on the situation.

"Very interesting reference to Atticus Finch, Mr. Matthews. Now, there was a man, as you said, that was very intelligent. But he was also a very honest man, a straight shooter you could say."

I had no idea where he was going with this. He casually strolled into my apartment, looked around, hands still behind his back. He nodded a few times and then said, "Not a bad place you've got here. Are you going to live here after you and Lily get married?"

He had my attention, and he knew it. Our eyes remained locked as he continued.

"I've always prided myself on being like Atticus Finch, a straight shooter. That's why I'm going to lay out before you a number of details so that you have a crystal clear understanding of the whole picture."

He went over to the arm chair, took of his trench coat carefully laying it on the back of the couch, and sat down. He left his gloves on and began to wring his hands very slowly, which produced that distinctive sound of leather being rubbed together. It was annoying to say the least. Finally he spoke.

"There's no doubt in my mind that you're wise beyond your years, and you're very loyal. You don't often see that in people. Now, I've got a job to do, and that is to apprehend a very dangerous criminal. You, on the other hand, want to protect this criminal because you don't believe he is what we've told you. As well, we are very concerned about the safety of your girlfriend and we don't know where she is."

I watched his eyes carefully. We still hadn't broken the lock on each others eyes.

"Now those pictures you were shown, disturbing as they may be, are the work of the man you know as William E. Brown, or Web as you prefer. He has been on our internal ten most wanted list, for almost twenty-five years now. The FBI has had a reward in place that I am authorized to offer to you. Now, there is a condition attached to this. Because of the need for us to move quickly in this situation, the offer is on the table for five minutes."

His last words caught me off guard. My innermost fears were intensifying. He looked at his watch and said, "Four minutes, forty five seconds." He kept staring at his watch, breaking the silence every fifteen seconds with, "Four minutes, thirty seconds. Four minutes fifteen seconds. Four minutes."

I felt I was up the proverbial creek, with no paddle. Should I bail, jump out and make a mad swim for safety, or should I drift along with the current? Realistically, there was no safe shore in sight. I'd have to drift along with the current. Damn it. Why so few options all the time? For now I'd have to appear to be going with the flow, and hope to be convincing.

"Just how much is this reward you're offering?"

Hastings' expression was one of those self satisfied looks, one of someone who just scored a small victory, but he wasn't the type to be easily fooled.

"A quarter of a million dollars, in cash. Not a bad wedding gift!" He looked back at his watch, "Three minutes, thirty seconds."

I hated time checks! What I needed was more time. Nervously I glanced at my watch. It was as if the second hand was racing. That's it! Lily! I'll tell him I'll deliver Web when Lily is back safe and sound! That will buy me more time. My deal was abruptly removed from the table. It had evoked a cold response from Hastings.

"I'm not here to negotiate. Three minutes."

I was out of ideas, and would soon be out of time. Hastings looked at Philips and Wallace and gestured toward the door. They both left the room. Wallace glared at me, shaking his head as he left. My heart began to race even faster, what was he up to? I was having a hard time catching my breath, and my breathing was labored. Yet Hastings sat there calmly looking at his watch, breaking the silence with, "Two minutes!"

His eyes remained fixed on his watch. My nervous anxiety heightened. I felt the only thing I could do was escape all this. There were two doors to my apartment, but they had them covered. What about up the roof? I had to come up with something fast.

Hastings raised his eyebrows and said, "Better calm down there, son. You're going to give yourself a heart attack. Remember you've got your whole life ahead of you! Oh yes, one minute, thirty seconds."

In my panicked state I blurted out, "I need more time!"

"That's something I don't have young man." He reached inside his suit coat pocket. Once more I feared the threat of a gun. Instead he produced an envelope, a very thick envelope.

"One Minute." He tapped the envelope repeatedly against the arm of the chair. I knew he enjoyed the anguish and frustration this heaped on me. I thought of a number of insults I would love to throw at him, but it would be futile. He was controlling the situation. The only control I had was my reaction. I was determined not to turn Web in.

"Look at that, times up. Here's your only option. This envelope contains fifty thousand dollars in cash, unmarked bills. Consider this a down payment on the quarter million you've been promised. You take this now and all you have to do is give us Mr. Brown's location, then once we have him in custody, you will receive the balance in cash."

Suddenly the door flew open. "Agent Hastings. A word with you, quickly please!"

It was Wallace. It sounded urgent. He remained standing in the doorway and Hastings got up to talk to him. Wallace leaned into him to whisper something. I strained to listen. As I did, I felt a lump come up in my throat. He was talking about Lily. What I heard added a further dimension to my increasing panic. "She was last seen getting into an older blue Chevy pick-up earlier this morning. Two witnesses said she was struggling with an older man."

My heart sank. Not Web, no way. Hastings turned around to look at me. He only raised his eyebrows, as if to send me an obvious message about Web. He turned back to Wallace and again Wallace whispered something to him, but this time so quiet I couldn't make it out. This had to be a set up. They wanted me to hear the first part. I had to make my move now.

I turned and ran full out to the back door. Just as I got there, one of the Agents posted outside saw me and went to open the door to grab me. My first instinct was to throw all my weight at the door and knock it back in his face. It worked, and dazed him enough for me to get by and down the steps. By now his partner parked in the alley saw what happened and came running over. He stopped at the bottom of the steps and raised his gun and yelled "FREEZE!" I was about five steps up so I did the only thing I could think of. I jumped and ploughed right into him, and down he went, hard. I ran to the side of the building to my car. I opened the door and Philips yelled out, "FBI! STOP NOW! GET DOWN ON THE GROUND HANDS BEHIND YOUR BACK!"

I froze. But only for a moment, then jumped into my car, fired her up and lit out of the alley. I was sure they wouldn't shoot, when suddenly a loud shot rang out. I saw Philips, he had shot into the air as a warning, but I wasn't about to stop, not now, it was too late. I floored the engine and sped away. I could see in my mirror the Tahoes starting their pursuit. There was no way they were going to catch me, not today.

Unfortunately I spoke too soon!

Shifting into third, I hit sixty miles an hour only to be greeted by an oncoming SUV with its headlights and grill lights flashing.

There was no mistaking who they were. It was the Feds. Smoke bellowed from my wheels as I slammed on my brakes, and came to a stop sideways in the road. I had underestimated the number of Agents that were in town. When the Tahoe came to a stop, three Agents jumped out, bearing arms. Now coming up behind me were the rest of the pack, uncomfortably close. Making good split second decisions was among my many weak points. But in next few seconds, I would change it for once. Just thirty yards ahead of me on the left was Hunters Lane. An old narrow lane way just over a half-a-mile long. I didn't think twice. The old girl left her marks on the pavement as I made my move. While this was my only possible getaway route, it was very narrow. I hated to take my car through it with the potholes and branches, then of all things. I was almost at the end of the lane way when an old pick-up turned into it and stopped. I clicked my headlights and held my hand on the horn. The dumb idiot! What would it take to clue in? I feared that I'd be on foot in short order. It must have finally registered because he started backing up, just in time. He cleared the lane way and I realized this was a blessing in disguise! It was Old Man Harper. We lived in the same building! I drove out of the lane way and pulled up beside Harper. I thanked him for backing out, and told him I had a proposition for him.

"When I get back I'll give you a hundred bucks if you pull back into the lane way right now and block it. I want you to stall those people after me. Just drive in, shut your truck off, lift the hood and pretend it won't start. Please hurry!"

"You got yourself a deal there Quint!"

Now, hopefully I would have a little more of what I needed, time!

For the moment, I had a little breathing space, so I'd have to make best of it. It was still daylight, and I had to find a canoe, hide my car, and get to Web. I wound through some back roads avoiding the main streets. I remembered where I could get a canoe! Norman's Bait Shop! Parsons Creek runs through the back of his property. I remember he had an old canoe. I made my way to his place. It was now after six, so he'd be shut. I drove behind his building and tucked the car out of sight. I got out and stood still, listening. No sounds of people or vehicles. All was silent. Hopefully I shook them off, for now. I was relieved that Norman wasn't around because he could never make a decision without his mother. If I asked him for his canoe, he'd have to go see his mama first! Now, find the canoe. I found it behind the shed in the yard. I took it down off the hooks. There were two paddles in it. I picked it up and walked to the creek. Would it keep water out? I set it in the water and watched for leaks. There were none. Thank goodness for small mercies. I took one quick look around; everything was still, no one was in sight. My escape efforts seemed to be working. I got in the canoe, and put the paddle to work. Finally, I was off to Web's cabin.

Chapter Seven

The cabin. I wasn't sure where exactly it would be other than the south side of the lake. On top of that, I had no idea of the distance. I wasn't sure how long it would take. Looking at my watch, there was only about three hours of daylight left. I worked hard at each stroke of the paddle, trying to cover as much distance as possible. If there was one thing I hated more than being on the water, it was being on the water, in the dark!

It took almost two hours to get to where the creek enters Parsons Lake. I stopped paddling and took a breather. I drifted under the old Bailey bridge, and as I came onto the lake, an eerie feeling came over me. It was much like in the movie *Deliverance*. The canoeists were looking up at the high cliffs, they sensed something was wrong, someone was up there. Much the same, I felt there were eyes fixed on me. I turned sharply to look back at the bridge, fearing the Feds were there. Despite not seeing anyone, a sense of panic overtook me. With a fury I repeatedly drove my paddle into the water, heading for the south shore. My hurried pace was taking its toll. I felt exhausted. The thought of not knowing where Lily was, added to the panic.

The wind had started to pick up. The lake had gotten quite choppy. Still no cabin I paddled hard against the wind. Then I saw a small clearing and a white cottage. But it wasn't Web's, his place had dark wood on it. Now the wind increased even more, whipping the waves even harder. I had to get off the lake, the water was far too rough, and the canoe began to rock. I dreaded the thought of ending up in the water. I had to head for shore and follow the shore line on foot until I came to Web's cabin. Paddling with a full head of steam I came up on the shore quicker than expected. The sound of the aluminum canoe hitting the rocks echoed loudly. I pulled the canoe up the shore and put it in the bush, making sure it was out of sight. There wasn't much light left, as I could see the sun starting to set. I made my way along shore, trying to negotiate the large rocks, and branches, and then, SLAM!

I had no idea how long I had been laying there. I opened my eyes, but found it hard to focus. I rubbed my forehead, then looked at my hand, and saw blood on it. Wonderful! I got up slowly, feeling dizzy. I just lifted my head slightly when I gasped what I thought was my last breath! Right in front of me a, pair of boots! Someone was standing over me!

"Oh man! You scared me!" I tried to stand up but started falling back He reached out and grabbed my arm. It was Web.

"How did you find me?"

"Easy. The sound of your canoe hitting the rocks was pretty loud. It's not often there's loud noises around here. Speaking of rocks, you've got yourself a nasty reminder that you found one using your forehead." However, he let me know he was unimpressed with my presence. "You might as well come up to the cabin, you know, the cabin I asked you not to come back to."

I didn't respond. I just followed him along the shore line for a short distance, then we reached his cabin. It was much closer than I realized. We went in and he told me to sit on the couch while he got the first aid kit, so he could patch me up.

I was extremely anxious to unload everything that had gone on. But the first order of business had to be Lily. I called out to him, "Do you know where Lily is?"

He came out of the kitchen, with a curious look. "Why are you asking me?"

Unbeknown to him, he had answered my question. I knew he had no idea.

"What's going on kid?"

There was so much to say, I was unsure where to begin. He had a concerned look as he sat down. He could read me pretty good.

"So, you've had your quality time with the Feds?"

"Yeah, you can say that for sure."

"Regardless, you still shouldn't have come back here, you should have waited 'til I got a hold of you. You know, they're likely honing in on us as we speak. We've got to move!"

"No! No way. I made sure to shake them off before I came here."

"How can you be sure?"

"I got away from them, hid my car, and got a canoe. I knew they were watching all the roads. This was the only way I could get here without them knowing."

"Well, kid, I've got some bad news."

My heart sank. I feared the worst! Was this to be a negative revelation? Were the Feds right about him? Web could read the fear in my eyes. Then with his squinting look, he explained.

"I'm talking about the Feds closing in on me." I felt some relief.

"One more thing, brace yourself, again. It's most likely they have Lily. Don't worry, they won't hurt her, they're using her as bait."

"Well they sure have me and her parents worried."

But why would he say they were closing in on him? I again stressed, "They don't know where I am. I hid the car, and used a canoe to get here, just like I said."

Web heaved a sigh. Without a word he stared out the front window. Then he looked at the door. He walked over to the light switch, and killed the lights.

"Why did you shut the lights?"

"Because very shortly we're either going to hear a knock on the door, or the door will come crashing open, courtesy of your friendly neighborhood Feds."

I felt a hundred pound weight had just been placed on my shoulders, along with the sickening feeling that after all this I may have led them right to him. How stupid of me to think I could outsmart Federal Agents. It didn't matter how sorry I was, I felt my actions had caused irreversible damage. Yet I wanted to know how. "How can you be so sure they'll show up?"

"Technology, plain and simple. They've got the latest hi-tech gadgets to track anyone, anywhere, any time. Tell me, what interaction you had."

I explained in detail everything that happened. "So when you went back to your apartment, did you change clothes, shoes, anything?"

"No, this is what I was wearing."

"Did any of the Agents touch you, rough you up, slap on the shoulder? Think carefully."

"No, nothing like that. Nothing."

"And you didn't take the envelope of cash or accept anything else?"

"No, wait a minute. When I got back in my car at the apartment, my cap was sitting on the passenger seat. I put it on when I got out at Norman's Bait Shop, but I remember I knocked it off when I was carrying the canoe on my shoulder. But I didn't pick it up, I forgot it there."

"Well it's a sure thing your car was bugged, and your cap. By now they've figured out the details about the canoe, and they'll have started further surveillance and the process of elimination."

"What do mean by 'process of elimination'?"

"They're going to check out every residence, cottage, cabin, outhouse, boathouse, whatever is along Parsons Creek, and whatever and whoever lives around this Lake."

I closed my eyes, and hung my head in shame and disbelief.

"For what it's worth, I am truly sorry."

Web's reaction to this latest development said a lot about him as a person, especially his calm demeanor in the face of adversity. His next words were very reassuring.

"It's all right kid. I know you tried to be careful, and you did what you thought was best. But I've lived every day for the past twenty-five years, knowing that one day, my past may well come a knocking on my door." He paused briefly then continued, "When you live with that expectation, you have to live in a state of readiness."

No sooner had he finished speaking, he abruptly turned his head toward the door. He whispered to me to be quiet and get down on the floor behind the couch.

I didn't move a muscle. An eerie calm filled the room. All was quiet, except the wind. I could hear it making its way through the tall pines with that familiar whispering sound. I lifted my head slowly. Web was standing by the side of the window, watching. He moved away from the window, and told me it was okay to get up.

"It's just the wind." He took a deep breath. "I'm going to tell you something, something about the wind. I've only told this to one other person a long time ago." A noticeably long pause followed, as he walked over to the window. "Like I said, I've only ever told one other person, someone very special, very beautiful." He stopped talking. I thought that there would be more. But I figured he had traveled back in time in his mind in the past, no doubt to a better time. Then he said it. "I envy the wind. It has no memory of where it's been."

I was unsure how to respond, sensing that was a deep connection to his past, one that unfortunately had a tone of regret. He changed the subject, abruptly.

"Okay, here's what we're going to do." He went over to the fireplace, and pulled the rug away from the stone base in front. "Now you've got to trust me. There's a small room under the floor here." He lifted up a section of the floor, about three feet wide. "I want you to stay down there for awhile. The Feds are going to show up, there's no doubt about it. Stay down there, no matter what, don't come out. Clear?"

"Yes, but what about you?"

"I'm going to get ready to greet them."

"What? How can you take on all those Agents?"

"I'm not taking them on. Not at all. I am going to try to talk my way out of this."

"How?"

"You'll see. I'll use a character I like. It's one my disguises. Now get down there, don't make any noise, and I'll tell you when it's safe to come out."

As reluctant as I was to follow his instructions, I accepted that he knows best. If he had lived all these years on the alert, in a state of readiness, who was I to question. He handed me a coat to keep warm. I got down into the small room, and he closed the lid over me. Not a real comfortable spot to say the least. It was cold, damp, and dark. I could hear him walk to the back room, and then open some drawers. After a few minutes he walked close to where I was and whispered, "I'm going to sit on the couch and read. Now remember, no matter what, you keep quiet." I dreaded the idea of being in this hole I knew it was around ten, and I was starting to doze off.

Suddenly my whole body jumped. There was a loud knocking sound. The Feds. It must be them.

Then I heard this other voice.

"Hold yer horses there!"

Who was that? It wasn't Web's voice.

"Who's that knockin'?" The same voice asked.

"This is the FBI. Open the door."

I could hear the squeaking of the door as it opened. But who answered it? I was about to find out.

"What in tar nation are you boys doin' at my door?"

"Are you Mr. Franklin Rose?"

"That'd be me! Only thang is it's Franklin 'D' Rose!"

"Do you have any identification on you?"

"What tha hell fer? I haven't dun nuthin'!"

"We need to see some I.D. to verify that you are Mr. Rose."

"Well jus' a cotton pickin' minute. Where da hell is that dum old wallet? Jus' a minute, I gots to find the damn thang!"

I now understood about his 'disguise'. His new character, or at least new to me, made me laugh, albeit a silent one, as he played his role.

"I'm a cummin'. Hold yer horses! Damn it! Stupid old wallet, ne'er use it! Here it is!"

He was very convincing as an absent minded elderly man. However, the small element of humor was about to be completely overshadowed. After he called out that he found it, I could hear a number of voices. Not the voices I would choose to hear.

"Mr. Rose, I'm Agent Wallace of the FBI, may we come in, sir?"

"Why sure ya can. Come and sit yer self down. I's jus' gonna have a snort of whiskey, care to join me?"

"No thank you. I need you to show me your I.D., sir." Web obliged.

"Is there anyone else here with you?"

"Huh?"

"I said, is there anyone here with you?"

"Sure as hell wish thar was. It's pret near dead quiet here all the time! It'd be kinda nice to have some female companionship once awhile, know what I mean? I remember there was this one gal, she come and..." Wallace interrupted.

"Have you seen anyone stop by here in the last day or so? Anyone at all?"

"Nope."

"Do you mind if us Agents have a look around your cabin?"

"Ya'll gots a Search Warrant?"

As soon as he said it, he burst out laughing with this crazy, dumb Ozarks laugh that even convinced me he must be more than a few bricks short of a load. Then he came back with, "I's jus' pullin' yer leg! Ya'll go head and looks around, but tell me, what ya lookin' fer?" I could hear a lot of footsteps. There must have been at least four Agents, with none responding to Web. Shortly after Wallace spoke up.

"We're looking for a Fugitive, and his accomplice. One's about seventy the other about twenty. Now they are very dangerous criminals, and we know they are in the area. Here's my card. If you see any strangers you phone me right away."

"Phone? Ha! I ain't gots no phone. Who I gonna call? But don't ya worry none. See that o'er there, that's ma Betsy. She's always loaded n' ready. She's so good she could shoot a match outta yer mouth at a hundred feet! Let me show her to ya."

I gathered he was talking about the rifle hanging over the mantle on the fireplace.

"That's all right. We don't need to see the rifle."

"Suit yer self. But that ole Betsy, she be lookin' after me. One time there was this here bear that come a strolling by, then took a look at me, started up towards me..."

"Thank you Mr. Rose, we'll be on our way now. We'll send an officer by here in the next day or so to check on you, and make sure everything's okay."

"Suit ya self. But I'd be jus' fine."

I could hear the footsteps as they made their way to the door. Finally, I could a little easier, or so I thought. Agent Wallace wasn't finished.

"Just one more thing, Mr. Rose. We ran a routine check on you, and I was wondering…"

Oh great! Here it comes, that damn Wallace asshole.

"You have only one bank account, no credit cards, no loans, no pension, no recent employment records, and yet you make regular deposit in cash to pay for the utilities for your place here. Where does the money come from?"

The first shoe just dropped! I feared the second wasn't too far behind. But I shouldn't have underestimated Web. He was quick on his feet.

"Well I reckon' I can tell yous 'cause yous beein' the law an all. I saved my money fer years, and I ne'er e'er trust them there banks. That's why I keep my money right here!"

I wondered what he was up to. I could hear steps near the fireplace.

"Jus' gimme a sec."

I heard an odd noise. It sounded like a stone rubbing against concrete. He must be taking a stone from the fireplace.

"There she be. Keep all them Presidents right here in ma trusty wool sock."

Thinking he had satisfied Wallace with his answers, again I tried to breath easy, which again was short lived!

"Actually, Mr. Rose, one more thing, sorry about this, but…"

No, not the other shoe!

"We cut your chain on the gate. Hope that doesn't create a problem for you."

"Hell no, don't ya fret none. I's gots lotsa chain. Ya'll take care now."

Finally, the Agents left. Web spoke to me in a very low tone. "Stay where you are kid, I'm here at the fireplace putting this sock back. They're likely watching for a little while so I'm going to start a fire and sit on the couch." I could hear the fire crackling, closed my eyes, and drifted off to sleep. I woke up to, "Okay Quint, you can come up now."

"Wow, I fell asleep. How long since they left?"

"About a couple of hours. The fire's gone out, and I turned the lights out so I could watch with my night vision stuff. Besides, I prefer a room with very low lights anyway. It looks they're gone now."

Web looked as if he was in pain. He rubbed his chest, went in the kitchen, and took a bottle of pills out of the cupboard.

"Pain killers?"

He didn't answer. But I knew he was in pain. He was leaning on the counter.

"I'll be fine in a few minutes." He took a bottle of Whiskey out of the cupboard.

"I'm going to have that Whiskey, or two!"

Now, more than ever, I had to know what went on in his past. I had to ask. After he chugged his second Whiskey, I was ready to take the plunge. I let a few minutes pass, hoping the drinks would make it easier for him to talk. The time came.

"Web, please. What's all this about? I mean the FBI? What did you do that's got their shorts in such a knot?"

He downed his third shot. He slowly rocked back and forth in the chair. Then, at last, he started to open a door ever so slowly.

Chapter Eight

"So, Quint, tell me something. How's your knowledge of history, say the last half of the 20th century?"

Needless to say, I wasn't expecting a history lesson. However, I wasn't about to stop him, not now. I gave him about as honest an answer I could, "A little less than average."

"Does the date September 18, 1970 mean anything to you?"

I searched my memory bank, to no avail. Nothing clicked. I shrugged my shoulders and told him it didn't ring any bells.

"Does the date July 3, 1971 mean anything to you?"

I gave a repeat performance. Web snickered and then smiled as he shook his head side to side.

"Okay, here's your third pitch. I'm sure you'll hit this one! Does July 30, 1975 mean anything to you?"

Nothing! Nothing was coming up on my screen. All I could think to say was, "Looks like it's a swing and a miss, strike three!"

"Well don't worry kid, you're not out! The rules of this game are a lot different. I wish they were as simple as good old baseball!"

I still had no clue where all this was headed. Leaning back, he took a deep breath, as he often did when he had something important to say, followed by one of those long pauses. He was obviously deep in thought as he stared down at the floor. Finally he looked up at me and said, "You're about to cross a bridge, one that you won't be able to 'uncross', if you know what I mean."

I did have a fair idea of what he meant, but regardless, I didn't want to stop him now! Quite anxiously I told him, "I'm ready!"

Even though I was relatively young and inexperienced in life, I doubted that very many people would have clued in as to the direction his questions were leading. But in the next hour, I was going to cross a bridge I never knew existed.

Web continued. "Well here goes kid. I going to start with strike three, July 30, 1975. That was the last day a certain powerful, influential union boss was ever seen."

Immediately a name popped up on my screen. "Jimmy Hoffa?"

He acknowledged my answer with only an affirmative nod.

What? Jimmy Hoffa? Give me a break, this can't be for real! I sat there in disbelief that Web was somehow involved with Jimmy Hoffa?

Web broke the silence.

"Now think carefully. We'll go back to strike two. July 3, 1971. Mean anything?"

I was clueless to the max. That's how I felt. I still had no idea. "I guess my history mark is below average!"

"Don't worry about it." That was reassuring. He hadn't given up on me yet. "This person had a very loud Anti-war voice, about American boys sent off to the Vietnam War."

He was letting let me think. He could tell I didn't have the answer. "To boot this guy was a music idol and polluted a lot of young minds." Again he paused, waiting for my response. Wasn't going to happen. I didn't know who he meant. Then he asked another question.

"Do you ever listen to music from the '60's?"

"Yeah, I do. I like a lot of that music."

"Did you ever hear the song, 'Light my fire'?"

"Oh yeah, I guess so, oh, okay. I get it. The Doors' Jim Morrison!"

I was pleased with myself, and Web gave me that silent affirmative nod. But what does this guy have to do with a date in 1971?

"Now back to strike one."

I wanted him to stop and help me connect the dots because I had no clue how all this was connected.

"Now think back, carefully, September 18, 1970, any bells starting to ring?"

No bells again. All I could draw were blanks. But Web was on a roll, and that was a good thing. On top of that, it was clear there were certain people and certain dates that were significant.

"To some people in America, this guy disgraced the American National Anthem." He watched my reaction.

"Man, you could be talking about any one of a thousand people!"

"Yeah but this guy disgraced the Anthem with his guitar."

Now that rang a bell! "Jimi Hendrix!" I got the nod! "Hey I like his music. I thought the Anthem bit was great!"

I couldn't help but wonder though, Hoffa, Morrison, Hendrix? What's the connection? I was still in the dark, he could tell.

"You don't see the connection do you?"

"I'm trying, but I just don't see where this all heading?" Then it hit me! The connection. it had to be! "They all have the same first name!"

Web smiled, "So, what's the obvious next piece of this puzzle?"

I thought carefully. Jim. Jimmy. "The Three Jimmies!"

"Bang on Kid." Web's tone was serious as he went on. "Remember the bridge? At this point you've only come a very short distance onto it. Want to go on?"

"Of course!" There was no doubt in my mind. He could tell I was extremely anxious.

"Now, for the next piece of the puzzle. What else do they have in common?"

Enough with the questions! Why wouldn't he just tell me and end my frustration! I didn't have the answer, so he filled me in. "Isn't it obvious? They're all dead!"

"Well I knew that. I just thought there was more to it than that."

"Actually, there is. There's a lot more to it than that!"

I thought my curiosity had peaked long before this, obviously not. It was climbing! Climbing steadily! More and more questions went through my mind. I stopped at this one, how or what does this have to do with a wedding gift for Lily and I?

Web was watching my reaction. He went back to 'the bridge'.

"We're going to coming up to the halfway point on the bridge, just so you know, it may get a little scary from here on."

Quite the chilling effect! I hesitated, even though I had been extremely anxious.

Fear had a grip on me, as if I was on an old rope bridge in the jungle, with the bridge swaying from side to side, and a deep gorge below. The feeling made me freeze like the fear of an extreme height would cause me.

"You all right kid?"

"Yeah, of course."

Web's interrupting me, was like extending a helping hand, helping me to grip the rope rails of this bridge, and be able to get across. I didn't want to stop.

He leaned forward, resting his elbows on his knees gently tapping his fingertips together. I knew this to be a prelude to something important, and it was.

"Those three dates I gave you have another common thread."

A long pause ensued. during which he didn't make eye contact with me. He leaned back, keeping his eyes focused on the fireplace while he spoke.

"All three dates aren't just the day of their deaths, they're the dates each one was murdered."

I felt my body temperature plummet to a new low! I struggled with the barrage of questions flying around in my head. Did Web have something to do with this? Hoffa disappeared didn't he? Hendrix and Morrison, I thought they O.D.'d? I had to ask.

"I thought Hoffa disappeared and they never found his body or any proof he was killed?"

"No, they never found his body, that's true." Web still hadn't made eye contact with me, but he did keep talking. "Trust me, he's dead!"

Agents Philips and Wallace's description of Web began to echo through my mind. I was actually trembling at the thought of the picture they painted. But I still couldn't picture Web as a cold blooded murderer. "How do you know he's dead?"

He looked right at me and said, "Because I was there!"

There was something about the tone of his voice, something remorseful. At the same time, it impacted on me, what he just admitted. He was there!

"So, can I ask what happened?"

"Sure. It's quite simple. His time was up."

"What about Hendrix and Morrison, didn't they die of an overdose?"

"Well, indirectly, with a little help."

"Man, how do you know all this stuff? Were you—" I stopped. The answer was obvious.

"You were there too?"

"Right again."

He now looked down to the floor. This was a man who was not proud of his past. He hung his head. I remembered something he told me.

"You told me earlier that everything you did, you were following orders. You're being kind of hard on yourself."

"Thanks Kid, I appreciate the thought. But for what it's worth, I was telling you the truth when I said I was no murderer."

What he just told me sounded like a contradiction. I expressed my feelings.

"Yeah, but didn't you just confess to three murders?"

"Actually I didn't. If you recall I said I was there. I never said I murdered anyone. As a matter of fact I've never committed murder."

There was no missing the confused look on my face. He offered clarification.

"I did kill one person, and only one. But that was in self defense."

"So who killed 'The Three Jimmies'?"

"One of my co-workers."

"Meaning?" I was intrigued by this additional twist.

"Meaning there were always two of us in these situations."

"You mean there's more than three of these 'Situations'?"

As was so often the case, he chose silent mode. After taking a couple deep breaths, he leaned forward, and as I knew from before, something important was coming when he rested his elbows on his knees, and tapped his finger tips together. I was about to become one of the few informed persons, informed about things that, well let's just say, when he came out of silent mode, some modern day history would have to be re-written.

"The organization I worked for had a code name for me. 'The Groundskeeper.' When I came to anything that affected the good old U.S. of A., in any detrimental way to them, well that was my ground or territory. I was the one who had to make sure the problem was looked after. I was there at each and every 'Assignment' to make sure the deed was carried out. You could also call me a sort of 'Confirmer' because I made sure the assignment was completed, as in the subject had been taken out."

"How many of theses 'Assignments' were you on?"

"More than I care to say!"

"So, what about this person you killed in self defense?"

"I should clarify that. I was in the Korean War and did kill some of the enemy. But aside from that, there was only one, and I knew him as 'Porter', which was of course, his code name. Fitting name at that, you know 'Porter', someone who carries out some task. That's the name I knew him by. I never knew his real name."

He got up, poured himself a drink, then walked over to the fireplace and added some logs. He rested his arm on the mantle, staring into the fire.

"Whatever his real name was I'll never know. But what I do know is he was a man of few words, and definitely enjoyed his work, there was no doubt about that."

He finished his drink, and sat down. He leaned his head back, looking very relaxed. He opened up his past even more.

"The training I received covered every aspect of carrying out an 'Assignment' to completion. A lot of thought and preparation went into every one of them. Like the first of 'The Three Jimmies.' Porter and I flew over to England, different flights of course, back in mid-September 1970. I rented a room in Kensington, just a few blocks from where Hendrix girlfriend Monica had an apartment. On the eighteenth when Hendrix and Monica went to a party, Porter and I broke into her apartment and switched her sleeping pills for a more potent product. Then we left there and joined the party where Hendrix was. I took him aside and said I needed to talk to him. When we were out of view of the main group, Porter joined us.

Since we were dressed in everyday clothes, he didn't believe we were Federal Agents investigating his manager for fraud, regarding hundreds of thousands of Jimi's money. Even with our

I.D.'s he was hard to convince. We told him we had to meet with him alone at two in the morning, and wrote down the address on a piece of paper. He was to bring the paper with him, and not discuss any of this with Monica or anyone else. She could come back after an hour and pick him up. We weren't getting through to him, he was pretty gassed. He told us we were full of shit and to get the hell out of his way then started to leave. Porter grabs him, and throws him against the wall, telling him

"If you don't show up at this address at two a.m. we'll turn the tables on you, 'cause you see we're FBI Agents, that gives us permission to throw your sorry ass in some jail cell where no one will ever find you."

"That sobered Jimi up a bit. Sure enough he showed up right on time, two a.m. We had laid files out on a table, making everything look very official, talked to him about his banking, taking notes on everything he told us. It took almost an hour. Before we were finished we offered him a coffee. Of course there was more than just coffee in the cup. Porter had added some Seconal in with it. Actually he put about three times the norm, since we knew this guy could handle far more drugs in one dose than the average person. This Seconal, it was a barbiturate that was used as a hypnotic and a sedative. After he drank the coffee we told him it was time to leave, but to make sure when he gets home to take a few sleeping pills, to get a good rest and we'd be in touch later tomorrow. After that I walked him down to the street and stood back in an alcove as his girlfriend drove up, and he got in the car. Porter and I vacated the room we were in, each got into a separate cab, and went to two different Hotels. I stayed just long enough until the news hit that Hendrix was dead. I was on a flight out of the country within the hour, and Porter left that evening."

"Can I ask a question? Why would your people have to get rid of Hendrix?"

THE GROUNDSKEEPER

"Plain and simple, he affected young America in a way that stirred a lot of trouble. In the eyes of some, he disgraced the American National Anthem at Woodstock, in '69, when he got carried away on his electric guitar. That was pretty well the last straw. Leading up to that was his very vocal Anti-Vietnam voice. He affected a lot of young soldiers over there, and over here, affected the upcoming young soldiers yet to be drafted. Soldiers over in 'Nam, gobbled up his song, "Purple Haze." It was as if it gave them a high. How ironic, the song wasn't even about drugs. I remember back in Kensington, when Hendrix drove off with his girlfriend, Porter quoted a line from "Purple Haze," with a slight modification, "This ain't tomorrow Jimi boy, it's the end of your time!"

"Then there was the other Jimmy boy. Jim Morrison. Basically it was the same scenario. He had the attention of young America. A lot of them were being or about to be drafted, to end up in Vietnam. So, a guy like Morrison who was totally against the war, and extremely vocal on his Anti-Vietnam position, it wasn't long before he had the attention of the people I worked for. Add to his 'Nam criticism, his lewd stage antics, and lifestyle, well, he was just plain and simple, polluting young America. I can't say I was surprised when I got the assignment. Porter and I took separate flights to Paris, France, where Morrison was living with his girlfriend, Pamela. We arrived there at the end of June, '71."

"We picked the early morning of the third of July as the target date. Morrison and his girlfriend went to a movie the evening of the second of July. Porter was at the theater and purchased a beverage and some popcorn, and brought it to Morrison. Porter was dressed in a suit and tie, pretending to be the theater Manager who had recognized Morrison when he came in. The snacks were on the house. Of course the beverage was slightly laced, just enough to cause a stomach reaction a few hours later. When

Porter came out of the theater we went to Pamela's and broke in and hid. After they came home, it wasn't long until they were asleep, and we patiently waited, knowing Morrison would have the reaction and head for the bathroom.

    Sure enough he got up after midnight, and after he was sick, began running a bath. We waited until he got into the tub and was relaxing, then Porter and I slipped in. His girlfriend never even woke up through it. Porter quietly went over to the tub, put his hand over Morrison's mouth, and gave him an injection. That induced a heart attack within a few seconds, and that was it. Before Porter took his hand off of Morrison's mouth he said, "You ain't going to be lighting any more fires Jimmy boy, and maybe now you can break on through to the other side." Both references were to Morrison songs. I went over and did my thing, check the pulse, take the pictures, and vacate. Couldn't always get pictures, as in Hendrix case, but it was only twice, I never got pictures. Anyway, we quietly left the apartment, and looking back, the second Jimmy was the easiest assignment. You know they never did an autopsy on the guy. Add to that the fact that there were so many rumors surrounding his death like saying he was into the occult, and that he planned his death. Then of course the rumors that he faked his death and went to Africa. The guy even said after Hendrix and Joplin died, that he would be next. No matter what the rumor mill has to say, he was dead, that I'm sure of. Oh! If you're wondering about Joplin, we had nothing to do with her."

    He appeared quite drowsy as he finished. Then he perked up at my next question.

    "So what went down when you did Hoffa?"

    "July 30th, 1975. It was a beautiful day, warm, eighty-five degrees, not a cloud in the sky."

THE GROUNDSKEEPER

As he floated back, he began to relate details that would not only peak my curiosity, but would take me to other side of the bridge.

Chapter Nine

"July 30, 1975. That was a turning point, for Jimmy, for me, and for Porter. Let me explain. I always got a hold of Porter, when I received an assignment. He never knew how to get a hold of me. I'd get the instructions from my people, and then pass them on to him to get things ready. I never once met my contact. They would always let me know when they had a new assignment. They would place a specific ad in the news paper for a groundskeeper. The wording was always the same, so I'd recognize it. They would list a phone number, which was long distance. I would call collect, from a phone booth, the operator asked them if they would accept a phone call from, a Mr. So and so, and I would use the same name each time. They would always accept the call then ask me to hold, while they traced the call. Once they had the number they would hang up. Shortly after that they would call back to the number I was calling from, telling me they'd be sending some information in the mail. I would tell them to send it General Delivery, care of the post office in a small town in the area, and everything was set in motion."

"You mean you never met the people you worked for?"

"Nope, never did. They had to stay as complete unknowns. No loose ends."

"So you couldn't ever connect them to any of your assignments."

"That's the way they planned it. They decided the

assignments, gave the instructions, and nothing could lead back to them."

"Was each assignment, uh, like, taking someone out?"

"Yeah, definitely. I never knew who, where, or what, until I received the envelope from them. You know, when most people receive mail, it's either good news or bad news. For me, whenever I got an envelope from them, it was always bad news; someone had to go. In some cases it really was sad news. But I've got to tell you, back in '75 when I opened the envelope and saw Hoffa was the mark, well, I went cold. It had been years since an assignment brought out that kind of reaction in me. Actually twelve years to be exact. But Hoffa? I sat in my car, looking over the information package. My gut instinct told me something wasn't right. For starters, I had always received the same format for instructions, a picture, name, location, and date. Very simple, very brief, and hand written on a single sheet of paper. Everything was kept to a minimum. But this time there were two pages of extensive details about Hoffa, the mob, and the info was typed, and we were to bring in a third person. While I think of it, I have a word of advice. I learned on July 30, 1975 not to ignore a gut instinct. But that would be later in the day. Leading up to it though, I had my assignment and my instructions to follow."

"Do you think they told you to bring in a third person because that assignment was so difficult or complicated?"

"No. Believe me. I'd been on some very complicated assignments in the past, and on every one of them there was a picture, name, location, date, and one piece of paper with handwritten instructions."

"So what did you do?"

"I contacted Porter, same way I always did. When I met with him, I showed him the envelope, and didn't act any different than I would normally. I wanted to see his reaction. Up to this point,

Porter and I had been on, I think it was, thirty-five assignments. Only once before had he shown any reaction to the picture of the intended hit. This time he gave a repeat performance. He looked at the picture, then at me, and said, "You've gotta be kidding." I told him to read over the two pages. After reading the first page he looked at me and said, "This doesn't feel right. A third person?" He shook his head in disagreement, but I told him to read on. I think what clinched it for him, as it did for me, was at the end of page two it said, 'Two million dollars each.' The most a contract had paid up to that point was a half million."

He hesitated as he looked at me with that squinting look.

"There's a lesson here, beyond the one about gut instinct. The lesson is the greed factor. When the greed factor enters the picture in any given situation, it becomes a blinding factor. A person becomes blind to a lot of things when greed takes hold. I can't speak for Porter, but I know now, the greed factor got a hold of me. I looked at that two million as my retirement package. Anyway, we moved forward and everything was set in motion."

"Who was the third man?"

"No names, kid. His name is best kept out of the picture. But it would have been a lot harder to take out Hoffa if we hadn't had his help. You see, our people knew the mob had wanted to take out Hoffa, as far back as '63, and for years there were rumors of more possible hits. But then in '75, my people, who had access to illegal wire tap info, learned there was a multi-million dollar hit in the works, partly because of a leak in Washington about the court's decision on—"

He stopped talking.

"Ah, you don't need to know about that. Anyway, the rest is history."

"But why would your people get you to take out Hoffa, when they knew another hit was in the works?"

"Basically, they're very thorough, and very powerful. They wanted to be sure it was done, and done when they said so. To boot, they've always had anonymity, nothing they ever did would come back on them. Last but not least their timing would make it look like a mob hit. They were always good at getting fingers pointed elsewhere, away from them."

He got up and went into the kitchen. He took a note pad and wrote something down. I could tell he was in pain as he rubbed his chest. He was taking his painkillers, again.

"Shouldn't you lie down and rest?"

"No, these pills will do the trick. Just have to give them a few minutes to kick in."

As he leaned on the counter in obvious pain, I expressed concern about mixing the pills with the whiskey. He brushed it off, telling me he'd be fine.

All was quiet for those next few minutes but in my mind questions continued to pour in.

What happened with Hoffa? What happened with Porter? Where's Hoffa's body?

Finally he came and sat down, leaning his head back on the couch. He closed his eyes, and I was sure he'd go to sleep, but surprisingly he went back to where he left off.

"Jimmy Hoffa! Do you know what his middle name was?"

"Haven't a clue."

"Get this, his middle name was Riddle, seems fitting doesn't it?"

"You mean Riddle, like a puzzle?"

"Yeah, like a conundrum, and just think, the whole country would love to know the answers about Mr. Riddle! You wouldn't remember this you weren't even born, but there were thousands of bumper stickers those truckers had on their rigs, all asking the same question, "WHERE'S JIMMY HOFFA???" Now, it's all coming down to the finale. You're the one who's going to tell everybody what happened to Jimmy boy!"

Opening his eyes, he sat up, clarifying what he just said, "Well, not really you, I mean they're not going to know it's you, 'cause your going to remain anonymous for your own safety sake."

It appeared the whiskey and pills had loosened his tongue. I felt a sense of guilt knowing he was talking about things he guarded so closely. Yet curiosity can be a powerful thing, and it won over. I wanted to hear more, and he had lots more to tell.

"Porter, Porter, Porter! Why did you do it? You know, it was a real hot day when we were sitting there that afternoon July 30th, 1975, in the restaurant parking lot. You know the one that became famous that day, The Red Fox Restaurant. We got there shortly after one. Our third man had arranged for us to meet Hoffa around two thirty. Hoffa pulled in early around two, in his green Pontiac, and just sits there. About fifteen minutes later he gets out, slams his door, and goes into the restaurant. Porter was sitting in the back seat, to be less conspicuous, and was watching Hoffa with binoculars. Hoffa was using the pay phone. A couple of minutes later Hoffa comes out. I can still see him, blue pants and shirt, marching back to his car in a real huff. He never liked to be kept waiting; he was an impatient guy. He got back in his car and slammed the door a good one. Our third man showed up right on time, floating in the parking lot in that big Merc. He got out and went over to Hoffa's car and sat in the front seat. I had doubts this would go smooth. Hoffa had to be convinced to go against his better judgment. The convincing involved getting Hoffa to come with two Federal Agents, to be immediately put into the Witness Protection Program. What clinched it for us was he was told his family was being picked up at the same time because the Feds uncovered a multi-million dollar hit on Hoffa's wife and kids. The hit was planned to be carried out with Hoffa watching and then he'd be killed. At this point we realized a problem, Hoffa wasn't getting out of car to join us. We couldn't wait. We decided to go over to him. We certainly looked the part. Two Feds, white shirts, dark suit and ties, and of course shades. When we go to his car, Hoffa jumped out waving a .38 in our faces, yelling; 'How do I know you guys are for real? I was just talking to my wife on the phone, she didn't say nuthin' 'bout Witness Protection!' That was the first glitch! Pulling the wool over this guy was one tough deal. I'm surprised we pulled it off, and in broad daylight. When we showed our I.D.'s, it just distracted him enough so I could grab his gun, and Porter could stick a needle in his arm; what you would call an instant relaxant. Hoffa couldn't stand up, so with one of us on each side we basically carried him over to the Merc, and put in the back seat. In the process we banged his head, causing him to bleed. It's interesting the FBI dug up some witness that saw Hoffa get into a dark Mercury with three other people, that he was yelling, and that his hands were tied behind his back. So much for eye witness testimony, it's rarely accurate. Hoffa was unconscious, and we carried him with his feet dragging."

Web stopped talking. He looked tired, rubbing his eyes, and forehead. I was trying to put a few more pieces of the puzzle together, particularly about Porter and this third man.

The thought occurred to me that since things soured with Porter, could he be.... I had to ask.

"So was Porter working with this third man in some way?"

Web snickered. "No, not Porter. He was working for the same people I was. But there was a twist. It all boiled down to this, I was no longer an asset to this 'Organization'. What I had become was a liability to them. I knew too much, and when you become a liability to these people, there's only one way they deal with it."

"Did Porter try to take you out?"

"Yeah, he did try."

"Did he end up the same as Hoffa?"

Web went into a blank stare. No doubt re-living a dark episode in his life. After a brief silence he continued.

"When Porter and I put Hoffa in the Merc, Porter rode with Hoffa, and our third man, following me in my car. When we arranged all this we told our third man that the drug would wear off Hoffa in about an hour. We drove south for about fifteen minutes to the arranged location. In this secluded spot we stopped. Porter and I put Hoffa in the back seat of our car. It was then that we explained to our helper that the family was not actually being put into the Witness Protection Program, but only Hoffa, for now. He got pretty upset, very vocal about the fact that something smelled foul. He knew we had conned him into working with us."

Web smirked as he continued, "I guess we conned a con! That's classic! Then we assured him he had indeed helped the FBI, and that it would not go unnoticed in the event law enforcement ever tried to pin anything on him. But that wasn't doing the trick. He was really shooting his mouth off! So, we pulled out the big guns and informed him we had a list of all his family and friends, and that any leak of information about this and those people would find their way into the obits, and that was a guarantee! Without a word he got in his car, and drove off. Now we were on our way to finishing our assignment, or so I thought!"

"Porter?" I asked. He shook his head in the affirmative.

"When we left there we drove another twenty minutes to our second location. It was an abandoned factory where we had a clear view of the highway and side roads. By the way, the drug we gave Hoffa was no relaxant. We weren't taking any chances. He was dead within minutes of the injection. Imagine, a guy like him, his number finally comes up and he doesn't feel a thing!"

"What happened next?"

"We waited about ten minutes to make sure we weren't followed, and then went to our third location, another fifteen minutes away. A small ravine, very secluded. It wasn't 'til then that I knew for sure something was awry!"

Another pause. He gulped the last of his drink, then rubbed his eyes.

"We were slowing down to stop when Porter asked me, 'So what are you going to do with your four mill?'"

"He no sooner had the words out of his mouth, when he realized what he had said. We were supposed to be getting two million each. In that split second I slammed on the brakes and Porter hit the dash. I reached for my .45 before he could reach his. I stared at him in disbelief, then told him to hand me his gun, carefully with his right hand, since he was left-handed, and to get out of the car. A self preservation mode had taken over and I wasn't taking any chances.

"With my gun aimed at him I got out of the car, not taking my eyes off him even for a split second. I asked him, 'How could you?' But he never answered. I told him that I wouldn't kill him, but would leave him there handcuffed. Then in a firm strong tone Porter said, 'There isn't going to be any prisoner left here today.' I told him don't be a fool, he didn't have to die. But he wasn't going to co-operate. He stood there and said he was getting in the car, and don't try to stop him, because as it was, he said he had always done the killing, not me, and that I never had the stomach for it. I thought about what he said, and in the process lost my focus, for just a second, and then it happened. He reached around his back for his back up piece, and I had no choice. It was him or me, and I chose me. I put three bullets in him and he dropped on the spot."

Web sat there, staring at the floor. Obviously there was pain associated with all of this. Without a doubt, he was troubled over the incident. The silence of the moment continued as if he needed to remember Porter, with a minute of silence.

"I felt sick to see him lie there, bleeding. I knelt down, pushed his gun to the side, and put my hand behind his neck to prop him up. He was trying to say something to me. I could barely hear so I leaned down and put my ear close to his mouth. It was hard to make out what he was saying, but it sounded like, 'I guess that makes three jimmies.' Looks like that meant far more than I realized, which became evident when you and Lily went on the Net. Anyway, shortly after, that was it, he was gone. Always remember what I told you about gut instincts, if it doesn't feel right, it usually isn't!"

"What did you do with Porter?"

"There was no time to waste. He had been ordered to take me out, so there was no doubt he revealed this location to at least one other person, his contact, or I should say new contact. I dragged his body over to a thicket, and laid some brush over him. I had to get out of there as quick as possible before any unwanted guests showed. I laid Hoffa's body on the floor of the back seat, put a blanket over him, and drove off."

"Tell me something. Why would your people use Porter to get rid of you when Porter knew about as much as you. Wouldn't he, as well, be a liability?"

"I've wondered about that. Most likely it boils down to this, they contract Porter to get rid of me then they get rid of Porter."

"I know this may sound dumb, but is there no way you could go to the police with any of this?"

"Two chances, fat and slim! There's no way kid. This organization I worked for, they cross all the 'T's, and dot all the 'I's. Do you remember what I told you about being a cop?"

"Yeah I do."

"Well corruption knows no limits. My employer made sure my name leaked to the FBI. They now have a pretty thick file on me, full of trumped up crap, going back to the 60's, all courtesy of my previous employer."

"What kind of crap are they trying to pin on you?"

"Stuff you wouldn't believe."

"Like what?"

"Let's just leave it at 'The Three Jimmies.'"

"Come on, it's not like I'm going to broadcast this!"

Web smiled, and had a little chuckle. "At this point I should tell you 'The Three Jimmies', which I said was a wedding gift for you and Lily, is worth a lot of money."

I couldn't grasp how that would be possible. Who would believe this story? I didn't want to appear an ingrate, but I had to ask, "Do you think anyone's going to believe me? I mean, a nineteen year old kid telling the country what happened to Jimmy Hoffa?"

"They'll believe you, kid. Microfilm doesn't lie."

"Microfilm?"

"That was a detail I didn't mention. After Porter said that makes 'Three Jimmies', I decided to put the assignment photos for 'The Three Jimmies' on microfilm. I kept duplicates of everything I ever shot with my camera. When I mailed photos to my people, I always had duplicates."

"Why haven't you tried to clear yourself with the microfilm?"

"Plain and simple truth is it wouldn't clear me. It would only confirm what happened to certain individuals, and would still point the finger at me as the hit man. The Organization behind all this would go unscathed. Remember, I said corruption knows no limits, it reaches much higher than you could ever imagine."

At this point I felt selfish, again. I became concerned about my safety. Would I not be targeted by Web's people if I came forward? Web must have read my mind.

"Don't worry kid, you'll be safe. I've got that worked out."

A sense of relief came over me. Yet I was still very anxious to know what else had happened that day, and of course where Hoffa was laid to rest.

I asked him to take up the story after he left Porter at the ravine.

Chapter Ten

"With all the doubts I had about this assignment, it's a good thing I had planned an escape route. You know, there's an old saying that death always comes in threes, but that day I beat the odds. Barely! The whole deal with Hoffa already had too many glitches, and now there came another."

"Did you run into some of your people?"

"Yeah. There was no doubt, but I wasn't about to stop to make certain, I didn't need to. Porter was the only other person that knew the schedule that day. When I drove out of the ravine, I knew I wasn't home free. Not by a long shot. I got back to the highway. My escape route had included a short distance south then a turn off the highway to a side road. But the short distance I had to go proved to be a long ordeal. Part of the problem was, whoever Porter was dealing with now, would know where we would be, what we were driving, which meant I was a sitting duck. I had no choice but to put the pedal to the metal and boot on out of there. Sure enough, about a mile down the road I picked up a tail. At first I wasn't sure, so I slowed down to see if they would pass. They didn't. There were two guys in an old pickup, with cowboy hats on. They looked like a couple of good old boys. They stuck right on my tail, so I slowed down even more, and finally they pulled out to pass. I looked over at them as they went by and the guy in passenger seat looked at me kind of like he didn't expect to see me behind the wheel. He was using his CB radio. Needless to say my concerns rose to new heights. I was still about five miles from the side road I had planned to turn onto."

"What was with this side road?"

"It was part of my escape route plan. Two days before the assignment I paid a rental agency to have a car delivered to a specific spot just in case things didn't go as planned. Call it another feature of my self preservation plan. Anyway, I had been focused on the pick-up truck, but that proved to be a mistake!"

"What do you mean mistake?"

"I was so busy watching the pick-up that I never saw what was coming up behind me. All of a sudden the car lunged forward, and I almost went off the road. I looked back and there was this big rig behind me. He had rear ended me! It was no accident! I could hear the roar of his engine as he stepped on the gas. Black smoke poured out the exhaust stacks; he was coming at me again! I tramped the gas to keep ahead of him, but then I nearly hit the back of the pick-up! They had slowed down trying to wedge me in. I tried to pass the pick-up but he started swerving back and forth across the center line. I think I aged ten years in the next few seconds. Suddenly, I heard a popping sound, and my back window shattered. Someone in the rig was shooting at me! The only thing I could think of was to ram the pickup to get him out of the way. That didn't work. I nearly lost control. Then another shotgun blast from the rear! In desperation I shot at the tires on the pick-up. Took three shots before I got the back left tire, and let me tell you, all hell broke loose! The pick-up swerved sharply and flipped twice, and came to rest right in the path of this big delivery van. The van nailed him broadside! I hit the shoulder to miss the wreck, slowed down, then instantly panicked realizing the big rig was bearing down on me. I looked back and could see he hit the brakes as smoke surrounded his tires, then all of a sudden he jackknifed. His trailer slid sideways and ploughed right in to the wreck. Next there was this thunderous explosion. I stopped the car and got out. There wasn't anyone else on the scene. I wanted to help, but hesitated. There was no way anyone could have survived. Just then another huge explosion. Flames soared into sky, with black smoke bellowing. There was nothing I could do. I got in the car and drove off. I only had a mile or so to reach the side road I had to turn onto."

"Did anyone follow you after that?"

"If my people had anyone else following, there's no way they would have got by the wreck. The rig, with its long trailer sideways across the road, blocked anyone from going by. It covered from one ditch, right across to the other ditch."

"So, were you home free now?"

"Not really. I didn't know what lay ahead of me. Remember, they aren't ones to leave loose ends. My main concern was to get to that side road and change vehicles, I was only a couple minutes from it."

He sat quietly for a moment. He looked very tired. I knew the combination of pills and whiskey had not only made him drowsy, but loosened his tongue more so as each minute passed. One thing I felt more certain about, he wasn't the picture of some cold blooded murderer the FBI had painted. I was surprised, but pleased that he continued with the story.

"You know the place where this accident was—"

He paused, and began to frown. A change in his mood was about to manifest itself.

He got up from his chair, walked over to the fireplace, and picked up a glass statue of a woman.

"Know this woman here? She's holding a pair of scales, scales of justice. Remember when I told you there's no real justice?"

"Yeah, I remember."

"Remember why?"

"You said because of greed and corruption."

"That's it. The prevalence of greed and corruption!" He held the statue up high and added, "And to boot, she's blindfolded. People actually expect that justice will prevail. What a joke!"

Raising his voice, he said, "The people I worked for, the scales always tipped in their favor. The blindfold they use is a see through model. They pervert justice." He took a seat, I hoped he'd calm himself, but that wasn't going to happen.

"Just think. Everything they did, they claimed was in the best interests of the American people. Well let me tell you, the only scales they use are scales of injustice," he yelled, hurling the statue at the fireplace, breaking her into pieces. He stood motionless staring into fire. He bent down and picked up pieces of the glass. Looking at the pieces in his hand, he continued his barrage against the organization. Though not shouting, his voice had a very firm tone. As far as what came next, I could never have imagined what I was about to be told.

"These people, they're untouchable! They have too much power. They arrange to take out a President!" he said, as he hurled a piece of the glass into the fireplace. "Take out movie stars," hurling another piece into the fire. "Union Bosses, ANYONE THEY WANT!" he yelled, followed by him throwing the remaining pieces of glass into the fire, with a vengeance. This was uncharacteristic of Web. However given the nature of his complaints, I could hardly blame him…but, taking out a President? After a short silence, he started talking again. His calm demeanor had returned.

"Interesting thought. That day the scales did somewhat tip my way, and what a laugh. All this happened outside Toledo."

"What's Toledo got to do with all this?"

"You know, Toledo Scales, they make weight scales. All this happened right near Toledo. But the scales didn't tip in Hoffa's favor that day, nor in Porter's. As far as the organization, they got two out of three. Number one, they got Hoffa. Number three, they got Porter. Good old number two got away. That's one of the few things I have the personal satisfaction of knowing, they didn't get me."

"So you made your vehicle switch next?"

"Yeah. Drove to the spot where the other car was. First thing I did was take pictures of Hoffa. Then I loaded him in the back seat, and threw some blankets over him, then put my extra gas cans in the trunk. I changed my clothes, traded them in for a pair of blue jean overalls, and put a full beard disguise on."

He started to laugh, as he told me what he looked like. The straw hat and overalls gave him the true farmer look. Then there was another surprise.

"Oh yes, I had a blonde ride with me."

"You had a woman riding with you?"

"Yeah, she was in the trunk of the car the day before. I didn't tell Porter."

"What?"

"Relax. It was a mannequin. She had a blonde wig on, bright blue dress, and dark sunglasses. You see if they had any of their people waiting down the road, just changing vehicles wouldn't be enough. They would be watching for a guy driving alone, not one with a good looking blonde in the front seat. I hoped she'd turn heads that looked at the car then I wouldn't have to meet any new people, know what I mean?"

"What did you do with the other car?"

"Yes, the ventilated one. She found her way to the bottom of the lake. That's why I picked that spot, very remote, a body of water, and no one around. I got some pictures of the car before she went in the water. It's all on the microfilm as well."

"Clear sailing from there on?" I asked.

"I figured they would have more of their people along the way, and they did. As the blonde and I drove about a mile south of the side road, a dark Impala with two men in it went sailing by, heading toward the wreck. Over the next few miles, two more dark Impalas were diving north, one of them slowed to check us out. I made sure to drive about twenty miles an hour below the speed limit, that way I'd look like an actual farmer, never in a real hurry. I also knew they would be watching every motel, gas station, and restaurant. But once I got past Marion, Ohio, I started to relax a bit. The further away I got, the less likely their tentacles would reach, as they would have a wider area to search."

"Didn't you eventually have to stop for gas, and something to eat?"

"I knew I'd have to eventually. But I had a bigger concern. It was getting dark, and driving late at night on some of those remote highways, you would often draw the attention of some totally bored State Trooper sitting at the side of the road. I kept an eye for a good spot to turn off to park for the night, and get some sleep. All of a sudden, when I looked in my mirror I saw a set of car lights that came out of nowhere. The car was really moving. I feared it was a State Trooper."

"Was it a Trooper?"

"No, it wasn't. The car came up to me real quick and passed me. As my lights shone on the car I could see three young punks in the back seat waving beer bottles. For the second time that day, I wasn't paying attention to what was behind me on the road. Sure enough a State Trooper was approaching, fast, with all the bells and whistles. When he passed me, there was at least some relief in that I wasn't the target."

He got up, and sighed as walked over to the window.

"It was too bad though, he was just doing his job, he was just a young man."

"What happened?"

"About a half mile up the road there was a sharp bend. I don't know exactly what happened, whether the punks lost or control or what, but the Trooper slammed into them. Another mess. I didn't want to stop, but as I drove by slowly, the Trooper looked to be hurt. The least I could do was make sure an ambulance call went in. I stopped and went over to check on him. He was bleeding, really bleeding badly. He was trying to reach his radio, but couldn't. So I told him just sit still and I'll call for an ambulance. He simply nodded. I put in the call and gave the location as best I could. I had just finished when I heard some loud voices. I turned to see two of the drunken punks had gone over to my car and opened the passenger door.

"Well, well, well. What have we got here? Looks like a real blonde cutie."

"The Trooper groaned as he tried to reach for his gun. I knew he was in no shape to use it, and by the look in his eyes I sensed he wanted my help. I asked him and he nodded. I yelled out to them to get away from the car and put their hands up. They completely ignored me and pulled the blonde out of the car, then roared with laughter. As I turned to confront the punks, my beard rubbed against the car door and as I placed my hand on the door, it pulled the beard enough that, well lets say it was no longer an effective disguise. Trouble was the Trooper saw it. Combined with my beard coming off, and the blonder mannequin on the ground, the look he gave me, told me suspicion found a place. But I couldn't leave him at the mercy of those punks. I told him I was reaching for his cuffs, and I'd make sure they didn't get away or hurt him. He barely nodded."

"How did the punks take that?"

"It was a big joke to them at first, until Mr. Smith and Mr. Wesson rang a shot off into the air. That got their attention. I cuffed the two together, and checked out the others in the car. The other two in the car were unconscious, but they had a pulse. I took the second set of cuffs and cuffed the two outside to their door handle. I went back to the Trooper. A look of suspicion was written all over his face. I came up with the story that I had been to a costume party and the blonde was part of the gag. It was only when I placed his gun back on the seat beside him he seemed relieved. I could hear an ambulance siren off in the distance, and assured him he'd be okay, which wasn't the truth. A few seconds later his head dropped. I checked his pulse, he was gone. I put the blonde in the car and left, hoping the punks' memory of me would be vague, to say the least. By the way, none of that is on the microfilm, it's just part of the story between the pictures."

"Where did you go after that?"

"I still had some loose ends. First I had to get rid of the rental car. It was just a matter of time before they connected the dots with the rental agency. The next town I got to that following morning had a small store and gas station on the edge of town. I wanted to get a newspaper for the Somerset area."

"Somerset, Kentucky?" I asked anxiously, thinking another clue had slipped. He didn't answer.

"I wanted to check out some cars. I had to get another one right away. I stopped in at the station. It was a typical old country store, squeaky floors and all. I grabbed a paper and paid the old man behind the counter. Then he said to me, 'Ain't from around these parts is ya?' I told him I was driving through on my way to Detroit to visit my sister. I wasn't the least bit interested in having a conversation with this guy and started to leave. The old man piped up, 'If yer goin' ta Detroit, yer headin' in the wrong direction.' Wonderful, now I had drawn attention to myself, exactly what I didn't want. I told him I turned around to come back to the store, which didn't wash. 'Ne'er seen ya go by, how long ago you come through here?' I told him just a few minutes ago. He just stared at me kind of strange. Then more hassle. A young girl about sixteen or so came out from the room behind the counter."

"Hey, I'm lookin' for a ride to Detroit. Got room for little old me?"

"She no sooner finished asking, when an old battle axe came out of the same room and yelled at her that she wasn't going anywhere. The old woman then turned to me and said, 'You dun here mister?' I bought a couple of chocolate bars, to change the air of question marks, and left, heading west 'til the next side road, just to make it look like Detroit was my destination. I found a phone booth and called about some cars."

"Did you still have Hoffa in the back seat?"

"Oh yeah, hadn't reached my destination yet."

"So what about finding another car?"

"Found a '69 Goat, nice dark green. Bought it off a kid who needed money for college. Told him I'd pay him what he wanted, if he went and filled her up with gas. That way I wouldn't have to stop and show my face and chance running into any more of my friends, know what I mean? Then I told him where to leave the car, and put the keys on the back left tire"

"Did you put Hoffa in the GTO?"

"Yeah, in the trunk, a lot easier since rigger had set in."

"What did you do with the rental car?"

"I found a spot that was suitable, not to far from there. It was an old dirt road that lead to a small lake. I never much liked the water, but sure serves the purpose when you want to hide something."

"Like a body?"

"Good one, Quint, but no cigar. Old Jimmy boy isn't resting in a watery grave. Water's good to hide something, but not good if you want something to disappear."

"So all this time Hoffa's body is in a car, and it's summer. Like, wouldn't he be starting to smell?"

"Not yet, but that's why I had to keep on the move to his final resting place."

"And that would be?"

"On the microfilm, it's all on the microfilm."

Chapter Eleven

"Speaking of microfilm, where have you kept it all these years?"

"Safe and sound, and temperature controlled. The location is here on this piece of paper."

He reached in his top pocket and produced the paper, folded in four. It was the one he wrote on earlier, in the kitchen.

I took the paper from him and thought, finally an answer. Now after all this time the secret would unfold. I anxiously opened the paper, and read what he'd written. I looked up at Web. The unfolding process of this secret was not as easy as I thought it would be.

"Is this a location?" I asked. "I mean, it doesn't mean anything to me." I was frustrated over what I felt could be a lot simpler, than using riddles, and puzzles, and mind games.

"Well, Quint, I've learned a lot of things in life, and let this be a lesson to you. One of them is be very careful what you say and what you put in print. Don't let be known what needs to be known until it's time. Think of it as, showing your cards, one at a time. Now I'm showing you one card. Read what it says, out loud."

"Hush, Hush Sweet Charlotte" and "The Stone Garden." I didn't have a clue what it meant.

"That's one card, now I'll show you another one, but first." He took out a match and set the piece of paper on fire, then stuck it in his glass. He took another piece of paper and wrote something down and then handed it to me. With even greater anticipation I read it, only to be returned promptly to my high level of frustration. Such Obscurity. But he seemed to be enjoying it.

"The Rock House? I don't have a clue."

Web snickered at me, as he took a match and burned that piece as well.

"You're probably not up on early American history. Let me explain these two cards I've shown you. The first one, I want you to think of a city."

I could only think of one. "Charlotte, North Carolina?"

"That's right. Now I want you to think what a Stone Garden might refer to."

I concentrated on his question. All that was coming to mind was pictures of rocks, rock formations, and the like. That's what I told him and he answered with, "Think beyond rocks and gardens. What has lots of stone, greenery, some flowers, and lastly, names spread all over acres of land?"

"A cemetery?"

"Yes. Now, you're wondering how does it all connect? I can tell by the look on your face."

"I guess that your enjoying this very much, I sure wouldn't want you to tell me anything outright, I would much rather you string me along, you know, keep me guessing."

We both shared a good laugh together. It felt good. It momentarily let us escape from the reality.

"All right then. Let's go back in time to 1775 in Charlotte, North Carolina. There was a Declaration of Independence signed, The Mecklenburg Declaration of Independence, to be exact. The main guy behind it was a man named Hezekiah Alexander, and the home he lived in was called the 'Rock House.' Now it's a historical Museum. When you go into the Museum, just as you walk in, it's like a Parlor, and if you look at the wall to your left, you'll see a number of oil paintings. Each of the paintings has a small brass plate under it, showing the name given to each. Take a close look at the one entitled, 'The Stone Garden.' It's an oil painting of an old cemetery. The cemetery was in Charlotte, and the painting dates back to the Civil War. Now the walls and trim and everything original in the house were preserved, and there was lots of heavy wood trim. To the left of the picture is some of that heavy trim. There's a piece of trim about a foot long that you have to remove, and once you have you'll see the framing for the walls. In that framing you'll see a hole drilled into the wood. In that hole is a cylinder like a tube. It's about an inch in diameter and about four inches long. The tube is made of stainless steel, and it has capped ends. Inside the cylinder, you'll find the goods."

"How can you be sure it's still there?"

"It's there. Historical sites like the Rock House are on what you could call a preservation list, part of the countries heritage and all. One more thing before I forget. You'll need a ladder, the picture is about eight feet off the ground."

I couldn't believe that as careful as Web was about everything, he wasn't worried about the microfilm. Likely my look of disbelief, prompted his response.

"You don't look convinced kid."

"That's right, I find it hard to fathom that you wouldn't take more steps to ensure that…"

He interrupted. "Let's just say I had a measure of control over painting."

"Control? How could you control a painting?"

"It was pretty simple. You see I went to an auction in West Virginia, a small town named Stonewood. That was way back in 1969. I outbid a woman whom I later found out was the curator of the Rock House Museum. She was very anxious to obtain the painting because the cemetery in the painting was part of the history of Charlotte, and was actually only two miles away from the Rock House."

More of the unexpected was to follow. Web had a very different kind of expression on his face. He paused for a moment, and surprisingly had a warm smile on his face. For the first time I was to see he had a romantic side. He related in detail how he became attracted to the curator. She had approached him after the auction asking if he would consider selling the painting to the museum, if she could come up with more money. Her sincerity appealed to him, and he agreed to meet her the next day and discuss it. His voice had a softness about it as he spoke her name, repeating it more softly each time he said it. Her name was Willow Hayden. He explained his control over the painting by the fact that he donated it to the museum, and stipulated that its location on the wall must remain exactly in that spot. Willow was happy to oblige. They began a relationship in the late spring of '69. It was at this point that Web took me back, back to the year 1969. He told me how different things were then. The country was abuzz about the incoming seventies. Young people had their summer of love, their Woodstock, and there were increasing protests against the war in 'Nam. John Lennon and Yoko Ono had their famous sit in, or sleep in, to protest against the Vietnam War. Then, his voice again went quite soft and low as he said, "And I had my Willow."

Web recounted the times they had together. He particularly remembered her favorite song, "The Look Of Love" which she had played over and over. She would tell Web she could see it in his eyes, and asked him if he could see it in hers, her beautiful brown eyes. Her hair he described like beautiful linen, and would tell her that Debussey wrote "The Girl With The Linen Hair" with Willow in mind. He would often call her my Queen of hearts. She was very refined, very delicate, and so caring. Her favorite Opera, was the "Flower Duet" which he said he still hears in his mind every time he thinks of her. Then, a look of despair came over him. He explained.

"Then came July 17th, 1969. It was not a good day. It was the last day I saw her. We were on a picnic by the Catawba River. She wept when I told her I had to leave. She wept bitterly when I told her I wouldn't be back. She begged for a reason. I told her I wouldn't lie to her, but that meant that I couldn't tell her anything. After that I had to keep her protected. There was one thing I did tell her, 'I envy the wind. It has no memory of where it's been.' You know, Quint, there are many pains in life, but among the most painful, is a broken heart. She was in a lot of pain that day. My Queen of hearts shed many tears. I loved her so much." He hung his head low. "I should have known better than to begin a relationship with her."

"Let me guess. The Organization?"

"Yeah, they definitely didn't approve."

"How did they know?"

"They knew. It was then that I realized working for them meant they had their watchdogs everywhere knowing my every move. However, one thing was for certain, I wasn't going to gamble with Willow's life."

"You mean they threatened her?"

"That they did. They got a hold of me through the regular procedure, and when I opened my assignment envelop, it was the first time it wasn't an assignment, it was a warning. It simply said 'Weeping Willow may have to be cut down.' That was on the 16th of July, the day before we went on our picnic. The rest you know."

"Did you ever try to get a hold of her?"

"No. You've got to realize they cover all the angles. The phones, computers, mail, everything. If I tried to contact her, they'd know, with their phone taps and the like. Anything I would have tried would have ended up the same; it would have raised a flag immediately. I bet they've listened in on her calls all these years, checking her mail, especially since I went into hiding. You know how tuned in they are, look at your search on the net for 'The Three Jimmies.'"

"I know what you're saying, but there had to be some way to reach her?"

"You know love is a word most people toss around, because they fail to appreciate the true essence of the word. They'll say they love this, or they love that. That they love this person or that person, yet if you truly love someone it means you'd be willing to die for them. So having said that, don't you think you'd want to protect someone you truly love, keeping them completely safe from harm?"

"I understand."

"There ends this lesson."

I didn't realize I needed a lesson on this; however, I had to agree with what he was saying. At the same time I could tell he wanted to shut the door on the matter of Willow. While this ended another sad chapter in his life, it made me think of how much I loved Lily, and how much she meant to me. If I had to pack up and leave, never seeing her again, that would indeed break my heart. I wondered though, since he had given me Willow's full name, why couldn't I look her up and contact her? As I sat there contemplating my next move, he, as so often before read my mind. He gave me that squinting look.

"You wouldn't be thinking of looking her up would you?" I hesitate.

"No, of course you wouldn't." He said with an air of sarcasm.

"Can I ask you another question?"

"That depends on what the question is."

"I was wondering, would Willow know you as Web?"

"Very good backdoor maneuver!"

I got the usual squinting, coupled with his don't go there look.

"You don't need to know my real name at this point. Secondly, don't even think about contacting her. I want you to drop that idea. It's history. It can't be changed or re-written. I don't even know if she's still alive. But I can tell you this much, since I joined this infamous Organization, she's the only one who knew my real name. Despite all my training to conceal my identity, I told her. She was special, so very special."

As he sat there I knew he was again, drifting back to '69. He appeared lost in the moment. Then to my surprise he drifted back even further.

"I've only been in love twice in my life. Willow, and my high school sweetheart, Natalie and that was a long, long time ago. Almost fifty years ago, all the way back to 1951."

The familiar hush returned. He was sinking deep into his memory. I grappled with the idea of whether to change the subject, sparing him some pain. Absorbed as I was with Hoffa, this microfilm, and his real name, there was something else he said. I was going over and over it in my mind. I decided to take a step in that direction.

"Remember telling me when you opened the envelope your temperature dropped when you realized Hoffa was the mark?"

"Yeah, why?" he asked cautiously.

"You said it was twelve years since an assignment brought out that kind of reaction. That would put it around 1963 right?"

The look he cast my way was very convincing. Convincing me that I shouldn't be asking. His response was very emphatic.

"Change the subject!"

Sticking my neck out a little further I said, "Well since I agreed to cross that bridge, I wondered about –."

Instantly he snapped at me, "That's a different bridge. Change the subject!"

Obviously I had steered into a forbidden direction. However, his expression did change, and he apologized, revealing that while some of his memories were precious, the majority were the darkest shade of black. The sad thing was, he said that though some were precious, they had pain attached to them. As before, just when I thought he was shutting down, he picked up where he had left of just moments before, back in 1951.

"Natalie, what a sweetheart she was. Dark brown, flowing hair, cute as a button. I wasn't going to let happen to Willow, what happened to my Natalie." An air of despondency has settled in.

"What happened to her?" I asked.

"It was late in 1950, winter was just around the corner. We started making serious plans. Then came 1951, and reluctantly, I was off to Korea. Then came the letter, the letter from her parents. The letter that broke me. The letter that told me Natalie died from injuries in a car accident. The letter that said she never regained consciousness, and died later in hospital. That was the letter that changed my life, forever."

Chapter Twelve

Web traveled back to January 1951, to the Korean War. As tired as he was, he still had more secrets, years of secrets, and the unfolding process continued.

"I was about your age when I ended up in Korea, nineteen years old and solid green. Korea was dead last on my last of places to visit. But I didn't have much choice. Uncle Sam called the shots. So there I was, around the thirty-eighth parallel, right in the middle of the Korean War. Any hope for a short stint vanished when the Chinese stepped in, and Truman reacted with there would be no retreat from Korea. Not very good news when you're anxious to get home."

As he continued, there was an angry tone in his voice; angry and bitter.

"Too much blood; too much death; everywhere. Then there were the snipers, those rotten little bastards were all over the place, and so were the damn snakes. You couldn't even take a crap without them cursed things trying to bite you in the ass!"

His feelings of resentment were quite evident. Resentment can often result in anger and hate. He would prove that true as more of his story unfolded.

"One morning out troop was at the base of this high ridge. O'Malley, our Sergeant asked for two volunteers to scale the hill and locate any nests. Machine gun nests that is. We had a lot of casualties in the last few days most of the guys were spooked, so there were no volunteers. Then O'Malley had one of his bonehead ideas. That morning I was off by myself, never did hang much with the guys. I could hear O'Malley, but wasn't within earshot to understand what he was saying. Apparently, when he asked for two volunteers he didn't get any offers. Then he yelled to me to come over to the rest of them. When I did he asked me if I was a coward. I told I may be a lot of things but I'm no coward. He said, 'I'll take that as a yes.' I had no idea what was up, 'til he filled me in for what I had just volunteered for. Then he picked another young kid, Trent, and told us he expected us back by dusk. I didn't like the odds I was facing. We were to scale the hill, on our bellies, and take out their nests. As we inched our way along, I kept thinking of Natalie, wanting so much to be back home with her. We would go a piece and then stop and study the ridge for any movement. Each time we stopped I took her picture from my shirt pocket. That was as close to my heart as I could get her. Then as we'd push on, the reality of war kept staring me in the face. The reality, that I might die right here in the middle of hell's hole. Trent was becoming increasingly nervous. He lacked the patience we needed to pull this off. I kept telling him to slow down. After some three hours, he spotted some movement. Slowly we came to within about thirty feet of the nest. We could hear them talking. On the count of three we each tossed a grenade into the nest and it lit up big time. Before I could grab him, Trent jumped and cheered and just like that, he was cut to shreds by another machine gun nest. He dropped to the ground right beside me. He was just a kid like me. I saw the look the in his eyes, the look of fear, the fear of dying. He died right there. A barrage of gun fire followed, they were sweeping gun fire all around the spot where we were. I still can't believe to this day, that I didn't get hit. Anyway, I laid there about a half hour without moving a muscle. I knew I had two choices. Make my way back to the troop at dark, or locate the other nest. My second choice had an obvious less likely survival rate. But it proved to be my only choice because if the troop had started up the hill, more of them would be killed. I knew the other nest was east of the first one. I worked my way back to the west, and came around the top of the ridge where I felt they wouldn't expect the enemy. Well, to make a long story short, I took out one nest and one more just further east. I made my way back down the hill, and thankfully the moon was out that night, which gave me a little bit of light to work with. From that moment on, when I got back to the troop things were set in motion."

"What do you mean, things were set in motion?"

"Set in motion, simply put meant the beginning of my recruitment. O'Malley took a special interest in me from that day on. He said I had something most guys will never have, and when the war was over, he knew some people that would have a job for me."

"What was it he said you had that others didn't?"

"Ah, doesn't matter now."

"Seriously, what did he say you had?"

"Just good instincts, stuff like that."

"You're playing it down, I mean come on you took out three of those nests!"

"Yeah, I might be playing that down some, but I'm not playing down what happened from there on. Our troop had a couple of close calls with snipers. As luck would have it, I spotted them both and took them out. O'Malley kept telling me I was being recommended for a medal, but I told him I didn't care about any medal. He said he'd send it to my parents. I told him my parents were dead, and I was an only child. All that I cared about was getting back to my fiancé in West Virginia. Well, I should have kept my mouth shut. Telling him that, was the mistake of a lifetime."

Web rubbed his eyes and forehead. He told me he wrote Natalie every week. But mail to and from the battlefield, was at best snail mail. Then he related what became the starting point for the sad and dark turning point of his life.

"By the time I got the letter about Natalie, her funeral was long over. So I missed her funeral, missed having a life together, missed a lot of things."

This was more of what plagued him, painful memories. But I had another question for him.

"How was that the mistake of a lifetime?"

"It wasn't until years later that I realized what a mistake it was. After I unofficially quit in '75, I moved around for awhile, never staying too long in one place. Then back in '77, I was driving through West Virginia, not very far from where Natalie had lived, how ironic that it would be near Langeley, West Virginia."

"Why would that be ironic?"

"That's the headquarters for the FBI."

"Right. But can I ask you something?"

"Sure."

"Is that where you're from, West Virginia?"

"No. I met Natalie there at her high school. I was from out of state and was there playing in a basketball tournament."

"Sorry for all the questions, I'm just curious. Please go on."

Web went on to relate how he always had a thing about walking through cemeteries, and reading the gravestones. He wanted to visit Natalie's to put some flowers on it. When he located her grave, he placed the flowers and saw that her father Reinhold Hoffman had died in 1964, but there was no gravestone for her mother. He decided to try to contact her, and was quite surprised she was still in town, at the same address all these years. He knew that as much as he wanted to, he couldn't go to the house and talk to her. Instead he phoned her pretending to be a reporter doing a story on longtime residents of Ripley, West Virginia. He had to get all family members names, and when she came to Natalie something didn't sound right. He related his conversation with Mrs. Hoffman.

"My Natalie was the most beautiful young woman, taken from us at such a young age."

"May I ask what happened to her?"

"It was a hit and run. It was so sad, she never regained consciousness."

"Did they ever find the person who did it?"

"No, the Police tried but never found the car or the person who hit her. Natalie was always a careful girl, who would never take chances with anything, especially crossing the street. A friend of mine saw the whole thing she was standing across the street. She gave Police a description of the car. She saw it because it was late afternoon, not night time like some people thought. My friend told Police she heard the car engine roar as it left a parking spot up the street, and that the car never slowed down one bit for Natalie. But the police said my friend was not a reliable, because she had had a nervous breakdown. That was the first indication they had Natalie killed."

"Yeah, okay, but how can you be sure they had Natalie killed?"

"Well the second indication was a little more convincing. I left the area next day and about thirty some miles from Ripley, I stopped for gas and bite to eat. While I was sitting in the diner a News report came on the T.V. screen. The scene was of a house engulfed in flames. The report then confirmed one person died in the fire, one Eva Hoffman, aged sixty-seven. The news said it was a gas explosion. I knew then that they had phone taps in place all those years, and since then, I've had her blood on my hands to."

"You mean they killed Natalie so they could recruit you?"

"In a word, yes. Keep in mind they couldn't have anyone on board with divided loyalties. Since I had no family, Natalie was the only connection I had to any other person. You could have only one loyalty, to them, exclusively."

"But why kill her mother?"

"A loose end. Simply a loose end, which my phone call had inadvertently revealed. How stupid of me. They probably used their voice pattern system, and that's how they knew it was me, and the rest, has now become another chapter in a book of painful memories."

"I got ask you something. How on earth could you ever team up with people like that?"

"I had no idea what I was getting into. Maybe it's just that I didn't care. When I got the letter about Natalie's death, everything changed. She was all I had to look forward to. The emptiness I felt, well let's say, I had nothing to live for. I became extremely bitter, was at odds with my troop, and took chances with my life that even shocked O'Malley. Then one night, he offered what he called a solution. I listened, and to make a long story short, it went like this, fake my death, send my dog tags home to be buried, nice gravestone, and a war hero's funeral. Meanwhile, I'd be sent to an undisclosed location, receive special training, new name, new fingerprints, and a new family."

"So, like you accepted all that without knowing what they wanted in return?"

"Naturally I asked what the program was all about. O'Malley said he couldn't disclose any further details, other than it would be one hell of a good paying job. The other thing he said was my next level contact would be a Mr. Colton."

"That was it? That's all he told you?"

"Yeah. I had nothing to lose. It was my ticket out of Korea,

I hated it there. The next day O'Malley sent me ahead to check out a dense wooded area. As he had explained that morning, I would be met by Mr. Colton, and was to go with him. There would be a pre-arranged explosion, and that was my death scene, May 19th, 1951. O'Malley took my dog tags the night before, and would pretend to find them at the scene, and that was it. Oh, yeah, except I asked about a body at the scene and O'Malley simply said, 'Way ahead a ya, it's all looked after.' So, everything went off as planned, met Colton, walked to a clearing about a mile away, got picked up by a helicopter, and taken to an air strip. Boarded a plane, took a long flight to somewhere in the Pacific. I slept through most of the flight, was treated like gold, and then landed on some island. What I really liked; it was warm and tropical."

As it turned out, Web explained he was on the island for about three years. He had received extensive training in what he called a long list of specialties. I asked what he meant. He said the list included military procedures, covert operations, similar to Navy Seal assignments, firearms training, particularly hand guns, and sharp shooting. He hesitated briefly and then continued with the list.

"And one hell of a list of lethal cocktails."

"What do you mean?"

"You know what Potassium Chloride is?"

"No I don't."

"It's a substance that's found naturally in the body. However, a large dose will induce an instant heart attack. And unless you're specifically looking for it, the cause of those deaths would be listed as heart attack."

After his three years at that location, he was moved to another island. He was given another plane ride. The additional training he received included, new identities, how to disappear, how to blend in with society, reactionary analysis, and numerous other types of mind games. This second stopover in his training lasted just under three years, and then he was given a final series of tests in all the areas he had been trained. He began to describe some of the tests then stopped.

"That's enough. Enough of that crap. Right now we need to focus on getting you safely out of here."

"Where to?"

"To get you back home, back to Lily and away from me."

"But what about you?"

"I'll be on the move in another direction."

"Where to?"

"Enough with the questions. You catch some shut-eye. It's almost four in the morning."

Reluctantly, I laid down to get some rest. When I awoke, it felt as if I hadn't slept a wink, yet it was almost seven in the morning. Little did I realize the events of this day would hold so much more of the unexpected. The unfolding of secrets had only just begun.

Chapter Thirteen

To my surprise, Web was not awake. He was still in a deep sleep. All was still. The sunrise brought a fresh look to everything as it lit up the room. As I sat there looking around, one had to feel a sense of deep sorrow for him. There were no pictures of a wife, kids, no one. His life had been taken away from him a long time ago. The only family he ever had was the Organization, the same people that no longer wanted him. It was no wonder he had a heart condition. How much can one heart take?

Pictures. There was one in the room, an oil painting. It was a beautiful scene, with a stream, a small waterfall, lots of flowers, and an old house. The caption on the bottom of the picture read, "Paradise".

This was probably Web's idea of the perfect place. I had to agree. I could feel myself being drawn in by the picturesque setting. I could hear the water cascade gently over the rocks. I could feel the sun's warm rays as I walked through the gardens. I could hear the songs of the gentle little birds. Looking at the house I imagined Lily and I sitting together on the porch, talking, laughing, and sharing our lives together.

The painting generated such a sense of peace, calm, and tranquility. I was lost in it. It had a magnetism like none I'd ever felt. I remained captivated by it for several minutes. I understood why Web would have such a painting. Unfortunately, it also reinforced a very sad aspect of his life. The painting wasn't real, but if only it could be, for his sake. It was unrealistic to think it ever could be, even in the future. For the present, reality was far from the peace and serenity that emanated from the painting.

Looking over at him, I could see he was still fast asleep. An interesting idea crossed my mind. I wanted to let it keep going, but my curiosity stood in the way. Since the "Stone Garden" painting was akin to some hidden secrets, what about this one? There was only one way to find out. Would it be an invasion of his privacy? There was no way to skirt that fact. My curiosity cleared the path. I removed the painting from the wall, and ran my hand around the frame. Nothing out of the ordinary, except there was a backing on the painting, held by four tabs. I thought most oils didn't have a backing, but rather an open back. I reasoned, if I had come this far, I might as well go the distance.

They say surprises come in small packages. Whoever "they" are, they're right. As I removed the backing there was a brown envelope between the canvas and the hardboard backing. It was unsealed. Without a doubt, the invasion was moving forward. I justified looking in the envelope for the reason that Web had already revealed many things to me. Lame excuse, but it worked for me.

Inside the brown envelope was a smaller white one. It was also unsealed. On the front it read "To My Love". I looked inside it, and found a handwritten letter and two black and white photographs. The first was a picture of young woman, very attractive, and the second one was the same woman, with Web, a much younger Web. This must be willow! The letter! Slowly I unfolded it then hesitated. This was crossing the line. Despite my burning curiosity, I would only look at the names in the letter, hoping to learn Web's real name. I took a quick look, and it was indeed signed by Willow, but addressed to "My Love". I gasped as Web stirred. Thankfully he didn't awake. I folded the letter then wondered if there was anything else in it that might tell me more. The invasion proceeded, despite the guilt I was feeling. The letter was dated, May 31, 1969. It read:

> To My Love: "Together Always.....Always Together"
> "My Dearest love. How my heart aches when we're apart. Each time I'm with you, it's as if the door is closed to the rest of the world, and there's only you and I. There could never be another for me. I cherish every moment with you. My heart beats only for you. When I look into your eyes, forever I can see. From the first moment you touched my hand, there was a warmth that entered my soul, and there it has stayed, there it will always stay. From our first kiss, I knew why that warmth was there. We were meant to be together always...always together. Each time we've gone down to the lake at night, the warmth from the fire, draws us close to it. Just as your warmth draws me to you. Please, let us always keep our fire burning. Remember, one day soon we will have our little paradise with our home, by a stream, with a small waterfall, surrounded by the beauty of our gardens. Please also remember my darling, that—"

I stopped. I had read enough. He was right about a broken heart. It pained me just to think about what they both went through. I understood how this painting would be something special.

After returning the letter to the envelope, I inserted it between the painting and the backing. As I went to hang it back on the wall, I noticed the wall bracket. What caught my attention was its unique design. I had never seen one like it. Putting the painting down, I focused on the bracket, which was a hinged type. Lifting the bottom portion upward, well look at that, there was a small round button on the wall. It was like a door bell.

Why would anyone have a door bell behind a picture on the wall, unless it was a—

My imagination stepped forward. Could this be some kind of switch? Maybe some kind of push button for a special compartment, say, something hidden? Sounded like a scene from a movie.

Regardless, there was only one way to find out. Since Web was still asleep, I allowed my escalating curiosity to win over, again.

I closed my eyes, held my breath, and pressed the button; nothing. Not a sound, nothing. Maybe I didn't press hard enough? I tried again. I pressed it harder and held it for a couple of seconds. I heard a clicking sound near the fireplace, and as I looked in that direction. I stood there in disbelief. A panel in the wall had just opened. It was a door. This was just like the movies.

I felt an extreme uneasiness about my next move. I approached the doorway very cautiously then stood still right in front of it. An open door, to where? I took a step forward. It was too dark to make anything out. A string from the ceiling hung near the door. A light? I tugged on it and sure enough a light came on. I looked around the room. In those few short moments I realized that I had walked right into Web's past!

I've heard many times that everyone has a least one or two skeletons in their closet. That never meant much to me, until, this very moment. This closet didn't have just one skeleton in it, it was full of skeletons. One cold chill after another, raced down my spine. Was this what his past was all about?

THE GROUNDSKEEPER

Often times what the eye beholds can send mixed messages to the brain, while the brain sorts through and tries to attach some clarity and understanding to what it has received. It was indeed a troubling message that was coming through to me. It left me with more questions and a very distinct coldness.

The room was relatively small. It was no bigger than four feet deep by about five feet wide. But in a sense there was a lot in this room. The wall in front of me, and both to my left and right were decorated the same. Three walls of photographs, black and whites, all of them about eight by ten. I knew some of the faces. On the wall in front of me was John F. Kennedy, Marilyn Monroe, Jimi Hendrix, Jim Morrison, Lyndon B. Johnson, J. Edgar Hoover, Jimmy Hoffa. On the side walls there was Lee Harvey Oswald, Martin Luther King, Charles Manson. Those were the ones I recognized. Yet there were so many that I didn't. Could Web have had something to do with all these people? The thoughts racing through my mind were very disturbing. I had to get out and close the door. This was too much to handle.

Oh my God! I jumped a foot! There was Web standing directly behind me, watching me. I was speechless.

A person's true character is often not known until it's put to the test. I had put Web's to the test. His reaction? Let's just say it was unexpected one. Instead of the long, silent, cold stare, or the familiar speech about backing off, he gave me that squinting look and a half smile. To my surprise, this opened door lead to another door about to be opened. With this turn of events, Web now began to relate details surrounding the persons in the photographs, details that would shock the country. Web had borne a burden few if any people would ever have to bear. Web's untold story was about to be told.

Chapter Fourteen

Web quickly dismissed my apology for invading his privacy. He told me this day had come sooner than he had planned. He walked into the room, and stood motionless.

"I call it, 'The White Room with Black Curtains, where the shadows run from themselves.'"

You might recognize those are lyrics from the song, *The White Room*.

"Why do you call it The White Room?"

"I really should call it the Black Room, with all its dark memories. But calling it The White Room lessens the darkness, and softens the shadows."

He remained standing in the same spot scanning the photographs.

"There's a mountain of pain and sorrow in this room that will never go away."

"Man, it's hard to believe there exist the kind of people you worked for."

"Oh they do, they're the type that have ice in their veins."

"They what?"

"You heard right. Ice in their veins. They're cold and heartless. A life means nothing to them. The only thing they care about is control. Achieve it at any cost, and maintain it any cost. No one is allowed to stand in their way. They trained us to have the same ice in our veins."

"How come they've never been exposed or found out?"

"They're a well oiled machine, extremely well oiled. Every detail is always worked out, no loose ends ever. They always make sure that attention is diverted away from them, so that someone else bears responsibility for their crimes. It's worked for a long time, and their still controlling, manoeuvering and manipulating virtually everything going on in this country. Yet at the same time it's as if they don't exist. They're perfectly cloaked."

"So do you actually know any of them?"

"I couldn't even give you one name."

"You mean you've never even met one of them?"

"Not one. Not ever."

"That's crazy. How can you work for some organization, and not know anyone there, or even where they are?"

"That's how they want it. But I have speculated some. They're likely from the Northeast part of the states. Filthy rich, powerful, and likely old money. I'd say a very small handful are running the show."

"Why do you think from the Northeast?"

"There's a lot of old family money in that part of the country. Same area where our founding fathers stem from. Anywhere between Philadelphia to New York."

At this point, still standing in the doorway, he reached for one of the photos. He took it off the wall, and gently caressed the face of person in the photo. It was Marilyn Monroe.

"Poor Marilyn. Such a beautiful person to be taken so young." He continued to caress her face. As he gazed at her picture he shook his head side to side. "What a shame to lose her, she was harmless."

He seemed to be quite taken with her. He continued standing there, caressing her face. I sensed his pain. I wished there was something I could do, but this was his painful past, no one could ever help him with.

"You know, she was my first assignment. I had just been given the code name, Groundskeeper about two weeks before that night. She was only thirty-six years old. August 5, 1962."

He began to relate the events of that night

"I was to get to her room by three a.m., and confirm she was dead. Take the photographic evidence, and leave. Well, I got there as arranged, but it was actually about two forty-five. Her bedroom light was on. She was lying on the bed face down, naked. I sat on the edge of the bed, and pulled a sheet over her. I took her right hand and checked her pulse."

He went silent for a few moments. When he spoke again, his voice quivered.

"A sick feeling came over me she still had a weak pulse. I sat right there holding her hand as the pulse got weaker and weaker. Then, she was gone. Right then a knock came on the door. It was her housekeeper asking if everything was okay. She listened for a bit, and then just left. She never even tried to open the door, or check on her."

"Why did they have to get rid of her?"

"Her fate was sealed when she hit the pillow with JFK."

"What do you mean?"

"There's dozens of theories out there. Most center around the idea that JFK, and his brother Bobby were consumed with her and likely were. It wouldn't take a rocket scientist to figure out that certain things may have been whispered in her ear, that never should have been whispered."

"Like what?"

"That I couldn't tell you. But what I can tell you is how we arranged the suicide that night."

"Who's 'we'?"

"Porter and I."

"Porter was there?"

"Yeah. It was the first time we worked together. As planned, Porter had broken into her house the day before, and replaced her pills with a more potent dosage. The instructions I received in arranging this, included a pill swap. My people obviously knew what prescription drugs she was taking. By increasing the potency, the combination of what she was taking would be lethal. Then, when I was sure she was dead, I put her original pill bottles back on the table, and took the ones that were specially prepared. There was no doubt they'd treat it as a suicide, and they did. I'm going to tell you something else about that night. As she lay there on the bed, I questioned whether I was cut out for this. I never wanted another assignment that would involve a woman. You know, I can still see her lying there. She was more beautiful in person than you can imagine. She was gorgeous, and harmless. She didn't pose any threat, she just happened to be with certain people at the wrong time. She got some negative attention. There's always been speculation that the Kennedy's had something to do with her death. But they didn't. The people I worked for, they saw her as a loose end, and the rest is history."

He returned Marilyn's photo to its place on the wall. He reached for another, from the wall on the right. It was the photograph of Lee Harvey Oswald. Staring at the picture he asked, "Do you know what Oswald said at the Police Station when they brought him in?"

"No, I don't."

"He looked right at one of the cameras and said, 'I'm a Patsy.' Of course, the entire country refused to believe him." He paused but remained focused on Oswald's photo. Without breaking his stare he said, "Poor bastard, that's exactly what he was. Only a handful at best, knew what was going on in Dallas that day, and even less who knew how it actually went down."

I was in a state of shock and disbelief at what I was hearing.

"You mean Oswald didn't shoot Kennedy?"

"That's right kid!"

"Then who did?"

"Well now, that hardly makes a difference after all these years."

"Sure it does. This country needs to know the truth!"

"The truth?" Web asked, then chuckled. "The truth, the good old truth, and nothing but? Well, let me tell you, the truth gets buried more than anything else on this earth. Dead bodies come a distant second. You know truth is part of honesty, and both are a rare commodity in this world, and non-existent with the people I worked for."

He returned Oswald's picture to its place, then went and sat down. But I had some nagging questions.

"Seriously, if Oswald didn't pull the trigger, then who did?" I couldn't let this one go.

Web took me back to November 20, 1963, two days before Kennedy was assassinated. In surprising detail he related what led up to the shots being fired from the sixth floor window of the Texas Book Depository. On the twentieth he and Porter got a hold of Oswald, under the guise of organizing the distribution of a large shipment of Pro Castro literature. It was mixed in with all the boxes of school text books piled high on the sixth floor of the Book Depository. On the 21st they verbally confirmed details about the shipment. They told Oswald not to report for work on the 22nd, but rather wait to be contacted. Early on the morning of the 22nd, they advised him to meet them at noon sharp, on the sixth floor of the Book Depository. That time was picked because all the workers would be getting ready to watch the President's motorcade. When he showed up, Oswald looked suspicious, until Porter started speaking to him in Russian, which helped put him at ease. There were some phony sheets of inventory, and box numbers to make it more convincing. The important thing as Web described it, it was to set things in motion within five minutes of the arrival of the President's motorcade. That obviously included getting Oswald's fingerprints on the rifle Porter had hidden, and make the timing just right to have Oswald in the wrong place at the right time.

Porter had the infamous rifle hidden in a long box. He took it out and showed Oswald telling him there were some firearms included in the shipment. He handed it to Oswald and asked him what he thought of the rifle. Porter pretended to reach for another one in the box. Oswald reached for the rifle then hesitated. When Porter showed him it wasn't loaded, Oswald took it.

As he stood there, holding the rifle, he began to frown. He looked at Porter, then at me. There was panic in his eyes. He smelled a setup. He abruptly handed the rifle back and said he was leaving. Handing the rifle back to Porter was our cue. I pulled out my .45, with a silencer, and ordered Oswald on the floor, hands behind his back. Porter loaded the rifle, and walked over to the window. He deliberately stood back from the window and balanced the rifle on some boxes. Oswald became very vocal, and quite loud, speaking in Russian to Porter. It fell on deaf ears. Porter took his position, and told me not to take my eyes off Oswald.

After a long pause, which may likely have been Web's minute of silence for the fallen President, he continued.

"To this day, I re-live that episode in slow motion. It still feels like a bad dream, a dream I can't escape. I still see Porter at the window shooting the first shot, then the second. I remember closing my eyes, knowing that the expert marksman he was, he would have hit the target. But then he fired a third shot which was not in our plan, and that threw me for a split second, breaking my concentration on Oswald. That was all he needed. Before I knew it he was up, and knocked me into a pile of boxes that crashed down all over me. Oswald headed for the stairs. Porter yelled out to him 'Go ahead take off. They're already looking for you!' Then Porter moved the boxes from the window area and hid the rifle behind them. Then we vacated the premises."

"How did you and Porter get out of there with all the cops around?"

"That part was easy. We flashed our fake Secret Service I.D.'s, and left the building before they locked it down."

"It was that easy?"

"Basically, it was. But it was also a matter of timing. Another interesting little tidbit about Dallas that day. I know there were quite a number of fake Secret Service Agents."

"So what about the theory about a shooter from the grassy knoll?"

"I can't be sure how many other teams like Porter and I were in Dallas that day. Only thing I know for sure, the invisible men behind all this, that we got our assignments from, wouldn't have left something this big up to two men. My guess, bare minimum four or five other teams were spread around Dallas. Since the wheels were set in motion, there was no way Kennedy would have lived past that day."

"Man-oh-man, I can't believe they set up Oswald for killing the President."

"They sure did set him up. He was the perfect patsy. Connected to all the wrong people, he had communist leanings, he was an easy sell to American People as the lone gunman who killed their President. Remember what I told you? When they set their sights on someone, they never miss."

"What about Jack Ruby? How did he come to figure into this?"

"Old Ruby, he did that on his own. Almost unbelievable the way it worked out. Oswald was going to be in Porter's sights, but Ruby acted before we did. Truth is kid, we didn't always get our man. Sometimes a guy like Ruby would beat us to it or other times the cops did like with this assignment."

He reached for the photo of Charles Manson.

"Now here's someone that adds new meaning to the word scumbag."

"You guys were going to take him out too?"

"Absolutely. But the Cops got him the day before we were going to pay him a little unfriendly visit at his compound."

He returned the photo to the wall, mentioning how when they found the little creep he was hiding in the cupboard under the bathroom sink.

He reached for another photo. It was Lyndon B. Johnson.

"L.B.J. Lyndon Banes Johnson. The man that sent thousands of America's young men to their death. He like so many others had a personal agenda. He wasn't going to let North Vietnam go unpunished. Doing so, also kept the war mongers happy. Then there was an interesting turn of events that took place one night, back on March 31st, 1968. At the end of his televised speech about the Vietnam War, he stunned his T.V. audience when he concluded his speech with a line that wasn't part of his script. He said, 'I shall not seek and I will not accept the nomination of my party as President.' He suggested there was a division in the house, and he was withdrawing in the name of national unity. As far as I'm concerned old LBJ knew something was up, since by the spring of '68 he wanted to let up on the North Vietnamese. He must have figured out that if he didn't want the same outcome as JFK, he'd have to pull in his horns, and step aside. To no avail, as it turned out. January 22, 1973, Porter and I paid a visit at his ranch. The goods were administered, and like so many others, it was ruled a heart attack."

"Why would your people wait, so long after he left the White House?"

"Can't be sure, but obviously our people felt he posed a threat with respects to revealing something that was buried, never to be unearthed." He returned Johnson's photo to its place.

"Can I ask you about another of the photos?"

"Go for it kid. I'm on a roll."

"What's Hoover's picture doing in here? Wasn't he, like, the boss of the FBI?"

"John Edgar Hoover, Mr. FBI. Yes, we paid him a visit too. They found old J. Edgar the morning of May 2nd, 1972, just the way Porter and I left him lying on the floor beside his bed. Interesting that they listed the cause of death as an undetected heart disease. Quite the character though. He collected a lot of dirt on a number of people, including presidents, four of which had planned to fire him, but never did because he held something over their heads. He also had a lot of incriminating information on other prominent people. Then all that came back and bit him in the ass. There's no doubt he gathered some information that triggered my employer to play it safe, and get rid of J. Edgar."

Aside from the photos he told me about, there were many that I didn't recognize. I pointed out one of them and his answer sent one of those cold chills spiraling down my spine.

"Did you ever hear of the Zodiac Killer?"

"You mean that guy is the Zodiac?"

"That's him!"

"I thought they never identified him?"

"That's true. The Police never did. But the people I worked for had a bead on him. They knew who he was, and Porter and I paid him a visit. We quietly eliminated him on August 8th, 1970."

"But how could your people know who he was? I mean the

police, didn't they have like hundreds of detectives working that case?"

"Yeah, the cops spent years trying to catch him."

"I just find it hard to believe your people could find this guy."

"They did."

"But why were they so interested in nailing this Serial Killer. I thought your people were more political. Why would they pursue someone like the Zodiac?"

"Well, there's a little more to that story."

"What do you mean?"

"When the Zodiac sent those letters, he used certain symbol combinations and codes. I recognized some of them. I had been trained to us some of the same codes. I knew that if I recognized them, then there's no doubt the people I worked for took note. I knew they would catch up to him, they had to, he was like a rogue agent. One of their own that went over the edge, so it was time to 'delete' him. I never expected I'd get that assignment. But I did, and like I said, we eliminated him."

"Man, that is unbelievable! These people you worked, it's just like you said, they have tentacles that reach everywhere."

"I've told you before, they know things. They know more than anyone can imagine. Always remember this, never believe that you have privacy. There's no such thing. Always guard what you say, whether on a phone, on a computer, or on a piece of paper. There is a 'Big Brother' watching, and listening. There ends this lesson."

"I'll remember that. But I was wondering, why wouldn't you tip the police off about this Zodiac guy after you did him in?"

"Not part of my assignment. I stuck to what I was instructed to do. No deviating. But I will tell you something that will rot your socks. This Zodiac guy, people think he was so intelligent and all that crap. Well, as Porter was about to give him his injection, he laughed, and told us, 'I'm only half your problem, you'll never catch the other half.' Sick bastards! The other half is still out there."

Web leaned back and closed his eyes. It was difficult, to say the least to digest all that he had served up in this short time. The impact was staggering, and to think, here I am, sitting in the same room with the man that holds secrets that people would give almost anything to know. Then again, there are people that would kill to keep those secrets hidden. Yet of all that he told me, there was one assignment that stood out, perhaps the most disturbing. I needed to express it.

"So Porter was the one who actually shot Kennedy?"

"He's the one. But I should qualify that. There were other shooters in Dallas that day. One thing for sure, Porter was a hell of a better marksmen than Oswald ever was."

"I thought they said Oswald was some super marksman with near perfect scores?"

"Any documents that showed him an expert marksman were carefully prepared as part of the set up."

"Man, they don't miss a thing, do they?"

"Like I said, a well oiled machine."

"What about that rifle? They lifted Oswald's prints, what about Porter's? Let me guess, gloves?"

Web snickered at my questions.

"That's one thing that was never a concern. I mean, it wasn't enough that we had our prints altered, Porter took it a step further."

"What do you mean?"

"It's very simple. Gloves. Porter never left home without them. Wherever he went, no matter what, he was never without his leather gloves."

My mouth dropped. My stomach turned. A sick feeling came over me. Web gave me a puzzled look, and asked, "What's wrong kid? You look like you just saw a ghost!"

Chapter Fifteen

Our mind will often play many a trick on us. It can imagine the best or the worst in any given situation. At that moment, mine imagined the worst. The gloves; the leather gloves. Could they possibly mean what I thought?

"Hey, you sure you're all right? You look pale. What's wrong?"

"Nothing. I was just thinking of something very bizarre."

"Well go ahead, spit it out. If it makes you feel that rotten, it's not worth keeping inside."

"No, really, it's nothing."

Web leaned his head back. In short order, he was asleep. I got up and began pacing back and forth, going over in my mind the things he told me about Porter, the last time he saw him, the day he shot him to death back in July '75. I can't see Web making the mistake of not ensuring Porter was actually dead unless, since he had to move quickly to get out of there. No, this thing with the gloves and Hastings had to be a coincidence, it had to be.

As hard as I tried I couldn't shake the idea that something didn't feel right. If I didn't say something to Web, and later found out I should have, I'd never forgive myself. I should ask him more about Porter, what he looked like, how tall, did he have a brother, maybe a twin? I had to ask.

Fifteen minutes went by. A long fifteen minutes. Then another fifteen. I couldn't wait. I woke him up.

"I've got to talk to you about something."

"Sure kid, go ahead."

"It's about Porter."

"Porter?"

"Yeah. When you shot him how did you know he was dead?"

Web looked surprised at my question. He gave me that squinting look and said, "That's an odd question, why are you asking it?"

"Believe me it's for a good reason."

"I put three in his chest. Nobody lives through that!"

"What if he did?"

"Hey, where are you going with this?"

"I just can't get it out of my head that the guy who was in charge with the Feds, Special Agent Hastings, might be Porter?"

"What? Now that's worth a good laugh. Where did you ever come up with that?"

"It's the gloves, the leather gloves."

"You've lost me, you'll have to explain."

"I saw Hastings twice. Once at the police station, and once at my apartment. Each time he had on a pair of leather gloves. He never took them off, not once, and he seemed to enjoy making that sound when leather rubs against leather."

Web shrugged his shoulders. "Is that what's troubling you? Listen, there's got to be thousands of people who wear gloves. I once met a salesman who wore cloth gloves, never took them off, until he went to bed."

"Still, there's something about this guy. He's real calm no matter what. Cool, calm, and collected. It's like he could see right through me, and knew what I was thinking."

"Put it to rest. Porter's long gone."

"Okay then, just humor me. What did he look like?"

"Just an average looking guy, you know, two eyes, ears, a nose and a mouth."

"Seriously, what he look like?"

"He was on the short side, about five foot eight, quite stocky, I'd say about two hundred and forty pounds. What about this Hastings?"

"He's about my height, six foot two, and on the slim side."

"Well there you go, that should be enough to convince you right there."

"Yeah, I guess so, but, what color was his hair?"

"Light brown, very little of it, and his skin was white."

"Now that's a relief! Hastings is as black as the ace of spades, and the guy is consumed with his favorite character, Atticus Finch."

Obviously I had panicked for nothing, or at least for the wrong reason. But the reality was they were still looking for Web, and they must still have Lily. I had to come up with something or someway to find out where they have her. Only Web could help me with this, but I couldn't jeopardize his staying in hiding. I noticed he had gone into one of the bedrooms. I waited but he wasn't coming out. I called out to him, "Do you have any thoughts as to where they might be holding Lily?" He didn't answer. I asked again. No answer. Finally he emerged from the room carrying a black briefcase. There was a pensive look about him. He set the briefcase on the coffee table.

"Well kid, it's time." I heard his heavy sigh, as he paused momentarily.

"It's a bit sooner than I expected, but here goes." He opened the brief case and took out an old type of binder, and three large brown envelopes.

"What do you mean it's time?" I asked.

"Remember what I told you, only a short time ago, that when the time is right, you'll have some of the answers you're looking for." He reached for the binder then turned it toward me. I sat down at his request, and opened the cover. He told me to read the name at the bottom of the first page.

"It says Hudson M. Stone." I looked up at him, and even though he hadn't said it I knew it must be his real name. I had wanted so much to know it, and yet now, I felt it pained him to reveal it.

"I guess this must be your real name?"

"That it is."

"But why are you telling me now?"

He didn't answer the question. Rather he told me to look through the pages. As I turned them, I saw they held newspaper clippings, clippings about Marilyn, JFK, Oswald, Hendrix, and of course, Hoffa.

"Why are you showing me this now?"

"Because it's time for me to move on, and I want you to have this."

"What do you mean, move on? Why?"

"I'll lay it out for you in black and white."

I was not prepared in the least for the next words that he spoke.

"The black and white of it is, when I described Porter to you, I used complete opposites in the description I gave you."

I felt a large lump in my throat. A familiar apprehension revisited.

"Oh man, say it isn't so!"

"Well, it is. No way around it."

"But how can you be sure it's him?" I asked

He gave me that squinting look.

"I'm sure it's him. Porter was about six foot two, slim, and definitely black."

"Yeah but, that describes half the black men in the country."

"True. But how many of them live and breathe Atticus Finch?"

I'm sure my bottom jaw came within an inch of the floor. How could that be possible? A flood of questions poured through my mind. What about twins? Maybe it's a twin brother? Or maybe just a younger brother? Web assured me that he couldn't have had a twin or a brother at all because as he had told me before, those recruited for the work they did, could have no living relatives whatsoever. Fear and frustration overshadowed my every thought.

"So where are you going to go? You can't just outrun the FBI."

"Oh, make no mistake, they're not the FBI."

"What? You mean these guys aren't for real?"

"They're for real all right. They're just not part of the FBI."

"So what are they part of?"

"They're part of the same Organization I worked for. You know, the guys who know things about everyone. The guys that function behind the scenes across this fine U. S. of A."

The impact of the last few minutes was like walking into a brick wall. There was no way to move ahead in this situation. I couldn't help Lily, I couldn't help Web, and my frustration had reached an all time high.

"So, what about Lily? If these guys aren't FBI, it means they're playing by their rules, and where the hell does that leave Lily?"

"I know. I know. Just hang tight. She'll be okay. They have no reason to harm her. They're working with the local Police, to make everything look legit. So don't worry, when you get back and I'm out of the picture, she'll show up."

"Out of the picture? To where?"

"You don't want to know. It's better and safer that way. Now, there is a couple of things we've got to go over."

He took the three envelopes, opened each one, and laid the contents on the table. Another unexpected turn of events came forward.

"These three envelopes are a wedding gift for you and Lily."

I was very thankful, but found it hard to think of our future wedding at a time like this.

"Do you remember when I asked you if you had three dollars on you?"

"Yeah, I remember."

"The first dollar is for this, I have sold you my house in town for one dollar, and this is the sales contract made out to you, Quint Matthews, and signed by me. The second dollar is for this, I have sold you this cottage for one dollar, and this is the sales contract made out to you, and signed by me. The third dollar is for this, I have sold you my '69 Yenko for one dollar, and the appropriate paper work is attached."

"My God! I can't take this! What are you doing, you can't just get rid of all this, and certainly not at the insane price of a buck! This is crazy!"

"No it's not. It's all legit. Now you take these three envelopes, they're for you and Lily. Call it a wedding gift, along with 'The Three Jimmies.'"

"Man, I don't know what to say. How do you thank someone for something like this?"

"You already have."

"But why are you doing this?"

"Well let's just say that you and Lily remind me of Natalie and me. We had our minds made up about each other long before I left for Korea. We had plans. Now all I have is a photograph. Take a look, here in the back part of the binder."

He took the binder from the coffee table, and turned to a section at the back. He showed me a page with a black and white photograph attached. It was a picture of Natalie. He turned the next page and it was blank. The reason it was blank, was the absence of the photograph he needed. He began to explain.

THE GROUNDSKEEPER

"This blank page, there's a photograph that belongs here, but I don't have it. There's a detail I left out of my story. Back in '77 when I contacted Natalie's mother, she told me something I never knew. She told me that Natalie was seven months pregnant when she was hit by the car. She was still alive when the ambulance got her to the hospital. Though she died shortly after, they were able to save the baby. The family kept it secret, because back then a child out of wedlock was unacceptable in most circles. The Hoffman's raised the child, a girl they named Margo, and told everyone it was their little niece. I tried to find out where this niece ended up. Mrs. Hoffman told me Margo eloped with a young man she knew in high school. She couldn't remember exactly what the young man's last name was. She knew his first name was Bill. The last name was something like Murdoch, or Murphy. She did get one post card from Margo, about a year later. It was post marked Vancouver, Washington."

There was an obvious question I had to ask. I was certain he expected it. Was he the father of Natalie's baby? I asked him.

His answer was yes accompanied by the regret that he never had a chance to meet her. He definitely made the effort to find her, but the trail went cold. He had gone to Washington to look for her. He did found out that Margo married one Bill Murdoch, and later divorced him. She moved to Denver, and later to Reno. But the trail went cold. After that it was hard to find any information.

"Did she just disappear or what?"

"No, she didn't disappear. I did find her eventually, but it was too late. Unfortunately she died back in '81. I located her death certificate and verified that most disappointing detail."

I thought to myself, didn't this guy ever get a break? Nothing but sorrow, grief, and sadness, that's all he's ever known.

Web took the three envelopes and put them back in the

briefcase, telling me to guard it very carefully. He told me there were some notes in there as well, and I should read them at a later date. He took the binder and put in the photo room. As he went to the wall to push the button to close the door he asked me, "So, did you read Willow's letter?"

I felt very sheepish, and guilty. I told him I had, and apologized. His answer was as usual, unexpected.

"To read another's hidden words can be an insightful journey."

I wasn't sure how to respond, and simply came up with, "I didn't read the whole thing. But it was obvious she loved you very much. You did have something special." He looked down and said, "If only life could hand out second chances. I'd be first in line."

Chapter Sixteen

When traveling down life's highway, as each of us does, there are times when we come to an abrupt halt. The reasons may vary, anything from an animal crossing the road, to a tire that blows. Something was about to cross my path, that would most certainly bring me to an abrupt halt.

Web went in the bedroom again, and came out with two duffel bags. He took one of them over to the fireplace, took the money he had hidden there, and placed it in the bag. I asked what he had in the second bag. He told me mostly clothes. There was no doubt he was planning to leave. The reality of the inevitable had arrived. It was painfully evident. I knew that Hastings and his gang were the reason.

"I guess your past has a nasty habit of trying to catch up with you?"

"That it does. Sometimes, like right now, it's too close for comfort."

"It's Hastings isn't it? Or should I say Porter?"

"Call him anything you want, but we'll never know his real name."

These past weeks I wanted so much to know Web better, and now, everything was coming apart. Coming apart, all because I set things in motion, looking for "The Three Jimmies."

"For what it's worth, I want to apologize to you, for setting things in motion, with 'The Three Jimmies.' I wish I could undo all the damage I've caused."

"Don't sweat it, kid. I've always said you can't un-ring a bell. What you have to deal with, deal with it. Speaking of dealing with, you know that through a process of elimination Hastings' people will be back here shortly. No one else around this lake will be a person of interest to them. I'll get the Yenko out of the garage, and we've got to roll. It's getting dark, and that's good."

"Does that mean I'm going with you?"

"No, I'm going with you. I'll let you know where to drop me off."

"What about all your stuff here? You can't just leave it?"

"Yes I can. When I sold you the cottage, all contents were included."

"But what about all the photos in that room?"

"That's all yours now. Come on, we can't be dragging our heels any longer. You drive the car, and let's go."

"Me? Drive the Yenko?"

"It is your car. Come on now. I'll tell you which way to head."

The only redeeming aspect of leaving was the opportunity to drive the Yenko. Off we went.

We were heading north on Highway Thirty-Five, driving under cover of darkness. A light rain had begun to all. I looked over at him and could tell he was very tense. He kept turning to look behind. A loud crack of thunder was followed by large drops pelting the windshield. I leaned over and turned the radio on. How fitting the song that began to play was "Rider's on the Storm."

As I listened to the words I watched him out of the corner of my eye. Some of the lines in the song troubled me. What if he isn't the person I believe him to be? Could he be as the song said, "A killer on the road?" Another cold chill greeted me as the song continued with, "If you give this man a ride sweet family will die."

Suddenly, out of nowhere, headlights appeared right behind us. I slowed to let them pass but they stuck right on my tail. Was it them? How could they have found us so fast?

If can't end like this, it just can't, not after all that's happened in these past weeks.

Web reached for his duffel bag. Surprisingly, the vehicle behind us pulled out to pass. After it sped by us, Web put the bag down. I'm sure he had a gun ready to use if needed. His demeanor conveyed a heightened sense of urgency.

"There's not much time, and there's more you need to know before we go our separate ways."

I hated the sound of that, but what could I do? The very least would be to help him escape the people bringing his past to the present.

The wipers had a hard time keeping up with the heavy downpour, prompting Web to suggest we pull over and let it pass. Time was working against him. We both knew his past was gaining ground on him. Fear and frustration had again taken over. It didn't help that we were on the only road that heads north to Baysville. However, his heightened sense of urgency included something I never expected. There was more he wanted to tell before he went his way.

"There's one more thing. When Natalie's daughter, Margo, died in 1981 it was a few weeks after she had given birth. The child was raised by the father's parents. It was much the same as Margo being raised by the Hoffman's."

That was something familiar to me. I told Web, "I can relate to that, I was raised by my grandparents as well."

Web looked at me, and in a low voice said, "I know you were."

"How did you know that? I don't remember mentioning it."

I was taken back by his comment, and at the same time, intrigued by it. But he didn't answer my question. So I asked again. "What you mean you know?"

Web turned around quickly as a car's lights came into view. We watched silently as the car slowly went by. When it was out of sight, he continued.

"Tell me what do you know about your family history?"

"Well, like I said, I was raised by my grandparents, the Matthews, and they never spoke much about my mom and dad."

"Why didn't they speak of them?"

"I guess it was too painful, since my parents died in a fire when I was only a few weeks old. Why are you asking me all these questions?"

He ignored my question again, and went on with another of his own.

"What were your parents' names?"

"My mother was named Maggie, and my father was Ben. Ben Matthews. Why?"

"Just bear with me. About your mother, what was her maiden name?"

"Let me think. Her name was—my grandmother told me. Uh, it was, Stein, yeah Stein."

"Sounds German."

"I don't know, is it?"

"The name Stein, is German, and it's pronounced 'schtine', it rhymes with fine, or mine. Do you know what the English word is for 'schtine'?"

"Haven't got a clue."

"The English translation is Stone."

"Hey, that's the same as your—"

At that very moment it hit me. I was in a whirlwind spinning round and round. Pictures, faces, photos, all took turns flashing up in my mind. Now the dots all had lines leading from one to another, connecting everything. I knew what my next question would be but it would be hard to get the words out. Web was looking out his window, not making eye contact. His silence confirmed what I had surmised. Now I understood why I felt so drawn to him. It was a moment that brought such joy, albeit temporary amidst the darkness surrounding us.

"You're my grandfather? You? Is this for real? I can't believe it!"

Web smiled. "I wish I could have told you sooner but I had my reasons. When your parents' house caught fire, your father, Ben, got you out of the house wrapped in blankets and placed you in their car. He ran back in to get your mother, and was overcome by smoke. They both died from smoke inhalation."

"How did you know all that?"

"I talked to your grandparents, the Matthews, Morgan and Irene, when you were only a few months old. I finally found your mother, Maggie, a name she chose to use after went to Reno. Like her birth name, Margo, both names are forms of the name Margaret. However the years I was looking for her, I had no idea she used the name Stein. I took for granted she was using Hoffman, and that's what made it so hard to find her. The Hoffmans being German, used Stein, instead of Stone. When I checked your mother's death certificate and saw her maiden name listed as Stein, I knew I had found Margo, but unfortunately, too late."

"You've known about me all this time, and never even tried to touch base?"

"Don't go there. What I did was for your protection. I was always around the area where you were living. The one time you all moved here, I moved as well. And since the Matthews are both dead now, I've watched you even closer these last couple of years you've been living on your own. By the way, did you ever wonder why your mother named you Quint?"

"Yeah, I've always wondered about that."

"Irene Matthews told me your mother named you after someone she really liked. An old TV western, *Gunsmoke*, had a blacksmith named Quint. That's where she got the name from."

"She named me after a blacksmith?"

"Yeah, she apparently had a crush on him when she was a young girl."

"Who was the actor?"

"Burt Reynolds."

"Burt Reynolds? Wasn't he that *Smokey and the Bandit* guy?"

"That's him."

At this point in time it was rare to find anything with even a trace of humor. But it did make me chuckle when I found out why my mother picked my name. I wondered what other information he might know about me.

"So what else do you know about me?"

"Actually right now it's more important that I tell you what else you need to know before we separate. Remember when I said you were going to be crossing a bridge? Well right now, you're a few feet from the end. You know the book with the news clippings I gave you?"

"Yeah, you put it in the hidden room."

"Remember what I told you about the microfilm about Hoffa? And where it's hidden?"

"Yeah. The museum."

"Right. Except that's only part of the package. The rest of the package includes where the body parts are."

"Body parts? You mean you cut the guy up?"

"Yes. But for good reason. His hands are preserved in Formaldehyde, and buried in one location. His head is preserved the same way, in another location."

"Why would you go through all that to get rid of the body?"

"Back then there was no such thing as DNA testing, there was only dental records, and fingerprints. Not much more than that to identify a body. There's a map buried in my back garden, in a stainless steel container, along with some other interesting information about Hoffa. It's two feet in front of the rose labeled, Charlotte. Now there's only one more thing you need. You need the name of the person to contact about 'The Three Jimmies.' Remember that info, particularly about Hoffa is worth a considerable amount of money. It's part of the wedding gift for you and Lily. This person is the one I tried to contact from the phone booth, the day everything broke open. Now, this person is the only one you can trust. When you talk to him, you have to say a specific sentence, and only if he has the right answer can you be sure it's him. His name is Carter Manning. He works for the New York Times. When you contact him you have to say this, 'It's time to open all the bags.' Remember he has to have the correct response, and that is, 'The cats have been in there far too long.' Have you got that? Repeat it back to me."

I repeated it back to him, and when I did, the reality hit home. We were done. The secrets that I longed to know were basically all revealed. I knew the time had come for me to let go.

"I'm going to miss you, to say the least. These few weeks of knowing you, wasn't enough. Is there any way we can keep in touch?"

"Tell you what. Always remember to look me up in *Webster's*."

I didn't understand what he meant. Why a dictionary? Before I could ask for an explanation he said, "The rain's let up. Let's move. Up ahead you'll see a sign that says Green Road. Let me off there, and you keep going."

"I thought you were going as far as Baysville?"

"No. They'll have road blocks set up ahead."

"You really think so?"

"They'll have every road going out of town blocked off, checking every vehicle going through."

"But, why Green Road? It doesn't go anywhere, it's a dead end?"

"You let me worry about that. Okay, pull over, there's Green Road."

Everything had happened too fast. He was leaving, and there wasn't a thing I could do about it. How I wished there was some way to keep in touch.

"Are you sure there's no way we could have some contact?"

"I told you, look me up in *Webster's*."

He grabbed hold of the door handle to leave. In desperation, I pleaded my case.

"Wait. Just a few more minutes, please."

"Time is not on my side, Quint. It has run out. Seriously, I've got to be on the move."

"Just, please, give me some direction or advice, as to where I go from here."

"Direction? Always go with your instincts. Usually you won't be too far off the mark. Advice? I'll try and condense this. Be careful who you trust. Never trust more people than the fingers you can count on one hand. Learn to read between the lines, there's usually a boat load of information and knowledge that resides there. Always remember this card, the same one you saw hanging on my office wall. The one eyed jack. Let it remind you that it's okay to be different from the majority around you. Be yourself. Your unique self. Not what others want you to be. Don't let too many people into your life, it makes things more complicated. And last but not least, marry your Lily. You'll never regret marrying the one you truly love."

He held out his hand to shake mine. His grip was firm. I could sense he was leaving with a strong determination to survive. I felt so helpless. There wasn't a thing I could do for him. He got out of the car, then leaned back in, and said, "I'm going to miss you kid." He gave a slight wave, shut the door, and walked off into the black of night. Much the like the dark world he's lived in most of his life.

Chapter Seventeen

I remembered Web telling me that the key to his survival all these years was to blend in with his surroundings. I had no idea what he had in mind this time, letting him off at Green Road. A dead end road, close to the middle of nowhere. Obviously he didn't want me to know.

I pulled away slowly, heading toward what would likely be a road block. About a mile and a half down the road, sure enough, there were the flashing red lights. I slowed down, and came to a stop. A trooper came over to my window. I rolled down the window, and he shone his flashlight in my face. He asked what my business was then asked for my driver's license. He took my license and brought it to another trooper, who then took it over to a dark sedan. The first trooper asked me to unlock the trunk. I asked why, which didn't matter, because he replied with the same order. I got out and unlocked the trunk, all the while watching the dark sedan. As luck would have it, Hastings and Wallace emerged from the sedan. I got back in the Yenko, and watched as Hastings came around the front of the car, and to make things a little more uneasy, he got in the front seat.

"Well, well, Mr. Matthews. I must say this is quite a coincidence to see you out here, alone, driving this car."

"What do you mean coincidence?" I asked, in an angry tone.

"Well, for starters, who would take a classic beauty like this automobile and drive it in this god awful rain?"

"I didn't know it was going rain."

"Secondly, we agents are out looking for a deranged criminal that you know and were with, I might add. Now, you show up at this road block alone?"

"What do mean I was with?" I asked.

"Only fifteen minutes ago, a driver told us he drove by your car and there were two of you sitting on the side of the road. Now there's only one of you. Would you like to tell me where you dropped of Mr. Brown?"

"Actually if you don't mind, I'm going to wait 'til hell freezes over."

Hastings gave me a cold, dark, penetrating look. But in his typical Atticus Finch approach to things he remained very calm. Down deep, though, I knew Web was in trouble.

"Well son, hell just froze over for your friend or should I say grandfather?"

There was no doubt that the look on my face gave it all away. As before, he had my attention, and he knew it. What was it with this guy? He's always one or two steps ahead of me.

"You see Mr. Matthews, Web, as you know him, is not the only sharp tool in the box. There's actually two of us. After tonight, you may well learn who is actually sharper."

Hastings got out of the car and called out to the troopers. He ordered four of the cruisers to head south and check out Green Road, because as he put it, it was the only side road between here and where a driver saw me pulled over. Hastings, Wallace, and one trooper stayed at the road block.

Hastings came back over to my window.

"You know Mr. Matthews, we may just have to charge you with hindering a Federal Investigation."

What a joke. He's not even with the Feds. But I wasn't going to tip my hand. It would probably be best if he didn't know that

I knew he wasn't with the Feds. The irony. He was on to me too. How the hell did he know that Web was my grandfather?

For a second time without an invitation, Hastings got in the front seat of the Yenko.

"Young man, you don't look very happy. You're probably wondering how I knew you were his grandson?"

I didn't answer. I wasn't about to give him the satisfaction he was looking for even though it was eating me up inside. Regardless, he wasn't going to let my silence prevent him from saying exactly what was on his mind.

"I see your back to your Boo Radley approach. Suit yourself. But I'm sure you recall me telling you that 'Every breath you take, every move you make,' and I believe I added, 'Every step you take' I'd be watching you. As you can see I am a man of my word. The watching process of course, included checking your background and what an interesting exercise that was. The reality, Mr. Matthews, is that we know everything about you, Mr. Brown, Lily, and anyone we set our sights on."

With his mention of Lily my silence was over.

"Where the hell is Lily?"

"Why, she's home, with her family. Thankfully she escaped from the location your friend Mr. Brown had been holding her captive. By the way, she's very anxious to see you."

What a bastard. What a bunch of lying bastards. They had her all the time. He sat there with a victorious smirk on his face. To say I felt a murderous hate for him would put it far too mildly, yet he was enjoying every minute of this. Still I had to keep a clear head. I thought of how Web would deal with something like this, and knew he would remain calm, and not tip his hand. I thought carefully on how to proceed, when I was interrupted by the noise of two helicopters overhead. As they hovered in whisper mode Hastings spoke with them on his radio. Soon they were off in the direction of Green Road. Hastings made sure I knew what was happening.

"Just so you know, we've also got a ground search going on in the area of Green Road. Three teams of Hounds are doing their thing, as we speak. Tell you what, you're free to go back to town and see your girlfriend. We'll talk more in the morning."

As much as I wanted to see Lily, I felt that leaving now would be like abandoning Web. I feared that if they caught up with him, they'd take him, and I'd never see him again. An even more disturbing thought crossed my mind. What if Web made it look like he had an escape plan, when in actuality, he wanted to be caught, knowing that then they'd leave Lily and I alone.

I watched Hastings talking with Wallace. Hastings again got on his radio. I could see a smile on his face as he listened. I heard him say, "I'm on my way." He and Wallace hurriedly got in their car, and drove off in the direction of Green Road. The lone trooper stayed at the road block. I was at a loss as to what to do. I felt so alone, standing motionless, hoping for some kind of miracle.

Miracles, of course, are hard to come by. I've heard about them, but never knew anyone that experienced one. I'd be a fool to think some miracle was going to change all that's happening. For now, I had to contemplate my next step. The first thing would be to drive back to Green Road.

When I got there I saw two officers with their cruisers blocking the entrance to the road.

As I expected, the trooper waved me to go on by. I wanted so much to know what was happening, but it was not to be. For now I desperately wanted to see Lily. So I drove to her place. I wasn't surprised to see that I had picked up a tail. They hung back, but I knew it was them. When I got back to town I stopped at Sandy's Deli, to get a sandwich. As I stood at the counter, I noticed the store phone. I had to call Carter at the New York Times. I asked the owner, and offered twenty bucks to let me call New York. He agreed. My effort to reach Carter was to be in vain. He was on vacation and wouldn't be back for at least three more days. So much for that. Off I went to Lily's house with my watchful friends tailing me.

Seeing Lily was what I needed. It felt as if I hadn't seen her for a year. I felt so close to her, more than ever before. She was shaken up by her ordeal. I asked her the obvious question, who did this to her? She said she never saw who it was. All she remembered was someone put a cloth over her face, and she passed out. Next she woke up in an abandoned warehouse tied to a chair. No one was around. A man with a dark hood over his face came in to bring her food and water, and let her use the bathroom. Then tied her up, and left. She worked at the ropes on the second day, and finally freed herself. That was it. Naturally I knew it wasn't Web, but I decided not to discuss anything with her, since they likely had her house bugged. I wanted to stay, but it was getting late, and she was exhausted. I told I would see her first thing in the morning. I had so much to tell her, but there was so little I could.

I left Lily and went back to my apartment. As happy as I was to see her I couldn't stop worrying about Web. If they caught him tonight, I'd never see him again. What did bring some relief was that, I still felt he was the sharpest tool in the box, and if anyone can stay hidden for twenty some years, that's quite an accomplishment.

I don't know what time I finally fell asleep, but it didn't feel like I slept at all, when a loud pounding noise woke me. Someone was at my door. I looked at my watch, it was seven thirty-five a.m. When I opened the door it was not the sight I would have asked for. Standing at my door were Hastings and Wallace.

"May we come in?" Hastings asked so politely.

"Do I have a choice?" I answered.

Wallace jumped at the chance to corner me. "Yeah, you have a choice, your apartment, or your favorite room down at the police station!"

I turned around and went to sit by the window. I pointed to the arm chair and looked at Hastings and said, "That's your favorite chair right there isn't it?"

He sat down, and Wallace sat on the couch. I stared out the window. I couldn't even look at these guys. I continued staring out the window and Wallace told me to look at them when they speak. I abruptly told him, "Up yours!" Hastings interjected

"Mr. Matthews we're here to let you know we have apprehended Mr. Brown. He is being prepared for escort to New York as we speak."

Without turning my head I asked, "Seeing him is out of the question, I presume?"

"You presumed correctly." Wallace enjoyed shoving that down my throat.

Hastings seemed rather quiet. I would have thought he'd gloat more than that. Regardless, I knew seeing Web was impossible. How I wanted so much to lash out at these, these frauds. I had to say something. I couldn't help myself.

"Who are you guys trying to fool? You're about as much FBI as I am the president of the United States. All I have to do is pick up the phone and call Sheriff Wilson, and tell him to phone the FBI in Langley and he'd find out there isn't any Special Agent Hastings or Agent Walleye or whatever the hell your name is."

It was evident by his expression that I was getting under Wallace's skin, but not so with Hastings. He sat there calm as ever, without the slightest change in his voice.

"Feel free to call Sheriff Wilson and tell him your concerns. As a matter of fact do it right now. Phone him up. Tell him to check us out with FBI headquarters."

He had to be bluffing. I was so convinced he was, I picked up the phone and dialed the Police station. As I was dialing, Hastings gave another speech.

"Keep dialing, don't stop. You go ahead and ask your questions, just bear in mind at this point, since we've zeroed in on your little town here we have, you might say, manipulated a few things. For example, the phone system, computer systems, and even a couple of those interesting satellites high above us. So everything, and I emphasize everything, is routed through our people. You may want to think very careful about that."

Think carefully I did. It meant that my call to New York was monitored by his people. Hastings hadn't taken his eyes off me. He knew the wheels were turning. Unfortunately for me, and Web, they were turning in the wrong direction. I slowly returned the phone to its cradle. I was extremely upset that I had tipped my hand when I called Carter Manning. Hastings next words confirmed the worst.

"We also came by to tell you that someone else you know met with an unfortunate accident. A Mr. Carter Manning, with the *New York Times*, drowned in the hotel swimming pool while on vacation. Such a sad turn of events. Now, to prevent any further such sad turn of events, there is one more thing. We feel it's quite possible that Mr. Brown may have shared some rather sensitive material with you. Information that is most certainly false. Nonetheless, it is still of a confidential nature, and you are not to discuss it with anyone. And I mean anyone. Period."

I couldn't believe it. My only contact and they got to him. What a bunch of sons a bitches! My options had run out. Hastings knew it, as he watched me carefully, with his fixed stare. He knew he was in control. His calmness was coupled with an air of confidence he thoroughly enjoyed conveying. However, he still had more to say.

"Let me put it to you this way so there's no misunderstanding. The watchful eye process that's been initiated especially for you, watching your every move is going to continue for some time. Even though I'll be leaving for New York, I've made sure that your going to be carefully monitored, and should there be, heaven forbid, any effort on your part to convey certain false information, then we will have to—"

"What? Some hired killer working for your dumb ass organization will take me out?"

He sat there wringing his gloved hands, enjoying the moment, with that arrogant smirk on his face.

"Hired killer is such a crude and harsh description. Actually, you'll be pleased to know we have graduated beyond such measures, to a more effective means to remove people from the ranks of the living. For the sake of simplicity, let's call our system one of mind control."

I was disgusted at the measures these people would resort to. My response was accordingly.

"I don't give a crap about your mind control antics or anything else you do."

"Actually you do need to hear this, and pay extra close attention to the intended lesson."

His cold stare had such an icy element to it. I listened as he explained.

"Mind control has been very successful for us going back some twenty years or so. Its proven results speak for themselves. We've gotten rid of a lot of trouble makers. Let me explain how it works."

He leaned forward in his chair. Obviously absorbed in what he had to say. His enthusiasm was not contagious.

"We recruit a certain type of person. Let's call him an unsuspecting fool. Then program him or her to carry out a particular assignment. The process takes some time, but as I said, the proven results speak for themselves. Take for example, Mark David Chapman. The voices he heard were the voices of our people as they programmed him to get rid of John Lennon."

My jaw resumed a familiar position near to the floor. I feared what was coming next.

"So, having told you all of this, it's important that you learn the lesson of which I spoke. Essentially it boils down to this, should you fail to remain silent about the details Mr. Brown spoke to you about, we will program some unsuspecting fool to fixate on your Lily. Over a short period of time we will have him convinced he must brutally murder her, because the voices he will hear, will tell him to do so. There it is in a nutshell. That's what you can expect in the event you make any effort to reveal any of that which Mr. Brown shared with you."

"Then I guess what he told me must be true, or you wouldn't concern yourself so much with it."

"Just remember, to be forewarned is to be forearmed."

If only there was some way to wipe that look off his face. Maybe the use of a question or two.

"Tell me something. If I ever need to get a hold of you, do I as for Special Agent Hastings, or should I ask for Mr. Porter?"

That touched a nerve, albeit for a few seconds.

The momentary silence was broken by the distinctive sound of his leather gloves, as he wrung his hands. While there was the possibility that he enjoys annoying people with it, it's more likely that he does it because he's deep in thought. A few more moments went by as he accompanied his hand wringing with his piercing stare. Finally he spoke.

"Mr. Porter. How interesting that you should pull that name out of thin air."

"Well it is one of the names you've used isn't it?" I asked.

"Now where did you ever come up with a cockeyed idea like that?"

For only the second time I felt I had his attention and it felt good. Perhaps I should take this a step further.

"Another thing. How did you survive three .45 caliber slugs to the chest?"

He didn't respond. All he did was sit there, wringing his gloved hands. I needed to take a different approach.

"You pride yourself on being like Atticus Finch, don't you?"

"One shouldn't ask questions they know the answers to."

"Okay. Deal. So I'll tell you instead of asking. You're not like Atticus Finch at all. He was an honest, straight shooter, whereas you, you're the furthest thing from honest. Plus, the only straight shooter connection for you is with a gun, or a needle."

Again, he didn't respond. It crossed my mind that I should use what may well produce the ultimate turning point. If nothing else, it might evoke a reaction.

"Speaking of straight shooter, you've never received any recognition for your expert marksmanship. I mean, those three shots from the sixth floor of the Texas Book Depository, that was impressive, even though it was only supposed to be two, it's still impressive."

It's been said that every person has a breaking point. As Hastings got up from the chair, I thought I was about to witness his. That was not to be. I may ruffled his feathers, but no more than that. His response proved it.

"My, my, you are one delusional young man. I have to say that you've been spending far too much time in left field if you get my drift."

His extreme calmness through all of this was exasperating. At least with Wallace I could tell he was biting at the bit to get at me.

Hastings no doubt sensed it, and asked him to wait in the car. When Wallace walked out he slammed the door so hard, a picture fell off the wall. It was a photo of Lily. Hastings used it to make a point about Lily. A painful one at that.

"You seem to forget that if your not careful, young man, your Lily may literally come crashing down."

"The same as you threatened to bring down a certain, 'Weeping Willow'?" I asked.

Endangering Lily was never my intention. The words about Willow just flew off my lips before I thought. I realized that in context, how would he know what I was talking about since Web knew Willow in '69, and he always got a hold of Porter for their assignments right up to '75? I watched his reaction very carefully. It was the same as it was to everything I brought up to him. He didn't ask for an explanation, nothing. That meant he knew about Willow, and if he did, that meant he must have played a more important role than even Web realized. This guy might be, or probably is one of the heads of this group or organization. Regardless, the cold reality of some harm coming to Lily hit home. I had said too much. I'd be much wiser to let him call the shots. And he did.

"Let me tell you one more important thing you need to know. Did you ever do puzzles, when you were a kid?"

"Yeah I did."

"Did you ever work on a puzzle and finish it, only to find there were some pieces missing?"

"Yeah." I wished I knew where he was going with this.

"How did you feel when you looked around for those pieces, and couldn't find them?"

"Well, you feel frustrated."

"So, what do you do with a puzzle like that?"

"I don't know, throw it out?"

"Let me bring this to the matter at hand. This puzzle you're trying to complete. There are a number of missing pieces. You need to be crystal clear on what I'm about to say. The missing pieces will never be found. So that being the case, you need to do with this puzzle, what every person would do with a puzzle that has missing pieces. Discard it, rid yourself of it. That is the only option you have."

He walked over to the door. Before he opened it, he turned and said, "Mr. Matthews, you're a smart young man. Don't resort to a foolish move. What I've warned you about you need to take very seriously. We aren't the type of people who give out second chances. You've been clearly warned. If you fail to heed the warning, you know what will happen."

Chapter Eighteen

Three Months Later
Three months went by very quickly. Lily and I were to be married in three days. Each day that went by I was so thankful for Lily. I was so fortunate that she agreed to marry me. I had all the reasons to be happy, and overjoyed. But truth be known something was missing. Something dampened my joy. It was not knowing about Web. I thought of him every day. I also thought of the unanswered questions that fell into the category of missing puzzle pieces, never to be found.

Through all that had happened three months ago, I never shared anything with Lily. I never brought up the subject of Web to her, because both she and her parents, and the Police for that matter, were convinced Web was the kidnapper. It's a very difficult thing to let a lie stand, especially such a terrible widespread untruth.

There was something else I hadn't told Lily. It was about the house, the cottage, and of course the Yenko. It was to be a surprise. I went to a lawyer and had the paper work done. Of course I had to clear it first with Hastings' men, two of whom had remained in town these three months. They were always around, dressed in plain clothes, trying to fit in. I was always aware of their presence. It was like Web said, "Big brother is watching and listening." However I had followed Hastings' orders to a tee. No communication of any kind about anything I was aware of. That wasn't easy.

I finished work at six and knew Lily had a final dress fitting. So I went home to grab a bite to eat. I was heating up pizza in the microwave when I heard a knock at the door. When I opened the door, I turned away in complete disgust.

"Oh man. What do you want now?"

It was Hastings, leather gloves and all, standing in the doorway.

"May I come in?"

"What the hell. As if I have a choice."

He came in and sat in his favorite chair. "So, just three days 'til your wedding."

"You came here to tell me that?"

"No, I came here for three reasons. First to let you know, these past three months you've been a good boy. You've kept quiet about all that requires your silence. Second, we let you keep the house, cottage, and car. We felt it was a suitable reward for all your help."

"Great. Thanks for coming. Can I get you anything? Hat? Coat?"

"I said there were three things."

"Well then let's get it the hell over with."

"Third, we have some unfinished business."

"What? Give me a break. What in the hell are you talking about?"

"It's time to break your silence." Hastings answered in a very quiet tone.

I didn't know what direction this was taking. I asked what he meant. He said the answer was simple.

"It's very simple. You tell us where Hoffa and any related information is located."

"What? Are you kidding? It's three days 'til my wedding and you come here with this?"

"You'll want to think about this carefully, and take it seriously, because no co-operation
by you means that you'll be missing your wedding day."

"Miss my wedding? What in the name of hell? Are you nuts? When is enough, enough?"

My outburst hadn't registered on him at all. He was oblivious to any of my concerns. He sat there calm as ever, wringing those cursed gloves.

Then he asked, "So, are you ready to co-operate?"

"What do you mean, ready to cooperate? Isn't that what I've been doing? Who the hell cares anymore about where Hoffa is? Why don't you just ask Web?"

"Actually we tried that, and when that didn't work, we tried Sodium Pentothal, which didn't work either."

In typical fashion, he knew how to get my undivided attention. I feared for Web. Feared what they may have done, and may yet do, if he's even alive. All I could do would be make the best of the hand I was dealt.

"Tell you what, I'll reveal what I know about Hoffa if you let me see Web."

There was no reply. As the silence of the moment mounted, a cold rush came over me. I realized that, again, I had pushed too far. He could turn the tables on me, and that's exactly what he did.

"Mr. Matthews, you should know by now that we don't negotiate. I only deal in black and white. You will co-operate. You will tell what we want to know, and lastly, you will miss your wedding day if you don't come through."

Deflated and defeated. That best describes how I felt. It seemed impossible to come up with a hand that could beat his. I would have to fold.

"Fine, have it your way." I said, reluctantly giving in.

"Now, wasn't that a lot easier? There's no need for you to be so obstinate. Just think of the positive side of this. For years people across the country have at one time or another wondered 'Where's Jimmy Hoffa?' They've speculated he's entombed in cement, or put through some rendering plant. Now, here's Mr. Quint Matthews, and he has the answers people are dying to know."

How I wanted to wipe that grin off his face. That smug, self-satisfied grin. But that wasn't going to happen. On the other hand, something didn't add up. I had to ask.

"Tell me something. Why is that you and your people are so intent on locating his body, after all these years? I mean, no matter where he's buried, what difference does it make now?"

"A valid question indeed. You're quite right to say that we are intent on locating his body We are of course not alone in that respect, since the FBI, the real FBI, shares that intensity. Nevertheless, there is shall we say, significant motivation to locate his body."

"Yeah, but that sounds ridiculous after all this time. What's there to find but bones, if in fact he's actually buried?"

"There are things that don't deteriorate in the ground, such as a small stainless steel container."

My eyes instantly locked with his. He baited me, and I bit. My instant reaction gave me away. Now he knew that he had something to sink his teeth into while I still had a lot to learn. Was this one of the missing pieces of the puzzle that Hastings spoke to me about? It's unlikely I'd ever know. Then again, was the container Web told me about the same as the one Hastings was looking for? It certainly appeared to be.

"So, Mr. Matthews. Let's make the locating of the stainless container our immediate priority."

I stood there silently, wanting to beat myself over the head. In a firm tone he asked, "Do we need to fly or drive?"

Reluctantly, I gave him the address of Web's house. He insisted I ride in his car. He phoned Wallace and told him to meet us there. We pulled into the driveway, and in behind us came "Walleye" and "Fill ups."

"Looky, looky," I said to them, "The three stooges."

"Well?" Hastings asked, ignoring my comment.

"It's buried two feet in front of a rose labeled Charlotte."

He passed the info on to Wallace who took a shovel out of his trunk and marched off into the garden. Phillips located the rose, and Wallace started digging. After about a minute we heard it. That unique sound of a shovel hitting something in the ground, something that doesn't belong there! Philips reached in the hole and took out a shiny container. He brushed the dirt off it and handed it to Hastings. Hastings surprised me with his next words

"Did it seem that soil was very easy to dig into?"

Wallace answered, "It did seem rather loose?"

Hastings cast a chilling look my way.

"Anything you care to tell us Mr. Matthews?"

I was taken back by the implication of his question.

"Hey, no way. Don't look at me. I've never put a shovel in the ground here."

Hastings prolonged his chilling stare. Without breaking it, he slowly turned the top of the cylinder, took it off, and looked inside. The three of us watching, stood motionless. What could possibly drive men to have to recover such an item? Hastings stood there looking into the container. What seemed like an hour, was really only a dozen seconds. He put the lid back on the container, ramming it hard. This had to be first! He nearly lost his cool. He quickly re-gained his composure, but as far as the atmosphere, well lets say the cold front that moved in moments ago, was intensifying. His next words confirmed it.

"Strike one, Mr. Matthews. That's a swing and a miss. The containers empty. What did you do with the contents?"

"I'm telling you, I've never seen that container before, and I certainly don't have the contents!"

Hastings went over and quietly conferred with Wallace, then came back to me.

"From our surveillance we've had on you these past months, it appears you have not set foot in this yard. I have little choice but to believe what you've told me. But I must warn you.

You play with fire, you will get burned!"

Hastings was not a happy camper. In a strong tone he took up where he left off.

"Now the next pitch is coming, Mr. Matthews. I want some answers. Your answer better produce a hit, and a good one."

I couldn't understand why the container was empty. Why would Web tell me what he did, when there were no contents in it? Something didn't add up. For now I had no choice but to tell Hastings about Charlotte.

"We're going to have to fly to point 'B.'"

"Where is point 'B'?" Hastings asked.

"Charlotte, North Carolina."

Hastings looked at Wallace and said, "Contact our people to get our Jet ready, A.S.A.P., and you, Mr. Matthews, just where in Charlotte would you be taking us?"

"The Rock House."

Philips piped up, "Hey, we have surveillance there."

Hastings shook his head at Philips. He obviously didn't approve of Philips remark.

I recalled Web telling me, they would be watching and monitoring that place and after all these years they were still watching and listening.

I attempted, in vain of course, to have Hastings hold off the flight until a few days after my wedding. Having failed that attempt, I asked if we could make an immediate return flight from Charlotte, once we had retrieved the information. How foolish of me to think that I would get an answer. He never responded.

By the time Hastings' plane came and we flew to Charlotte almost a whole day had gone by. Still Hastings would not let me contact Lily. How frustrating. I was extremely anxious to get this over with. However, once we go to the Rock House, there were still more revelations to come.

Chapter Nineteen

Hastings gave me explicit instructions as far as my role to be played as an advisor to the FBI on Historic American Architecture. Specifically; false walls, hidden compartments, and the like. Seemed a stretch at best, given my age and all.

However, I was more preoccupied with the fact that Willow Hayden may actually be there. I was anxious to meet her, if in fact she was even around anymore. Philips had let it slip that they had surveillance on the museum so Willow must still be there. It was hard to fathom that some thirty years after Web had contact with Willow, they were still watching and listening. They were relentless in their quest for Web.

We drove from the airport to the museum. It was near closing by the time we arrived, but Hastings' people had made arrangements for one of the staff to be on hand for an additional hour or so to assist us. When we arrived we were greeted by a beautiful young woman named Evelyn. She was tall, with dark hair, wearing a sleek black dress, which she assured us was not her normal attire, but rather she was dressed for a function that she would be attending as soon as we were finished at the museum.

Hastings and Evelyn went into her office, where as planned, she would hear one of his many stories about the "FBI." Wallace and Philips supervised my hidden compartment search. I made certain to follow Web's instructions exactly as he said. Using a stepladder I was able to reach alongside the very picture Web had given to Willow for the museum, 'The Stone Garden'.

The picture was still there. Willow had kept her promise to Web. Now of course the task at hand needed to be completed. Removing the trim, I looked and there it was. The hole drilled, just like he said, and a small cylinder. I took it out, and told Wallace I'd bring it to Hastings. Wallace insisted that I give it to him and stay with Philips while he brought it to Hastings. Arguing was pointless so I waited in the hallway just past the lobby. I noticed the wall plaques listing the different curators of the museum. I scanned them for Willow's name, and there it was. "In honor of twenty-five years of service. Presented to Willow E. Hayden. October 10, 1991." Just below the plaque was her picture. I recognized if from the one in the envelope hidden behind the picture at the cabin. My heart sank. Under the picture it read, "In Loving Memory of Willow Hayden 1935–1996."

I didn't even know her yet I felt devastated. Another sad chapter in Web's life. I went and sat down in the lobby waiting for Hastings. It occurred to me that if Willow died in '96 why would they still have surveillance on this place? Again it was pointless to try to figure out their reasoning. Wallace came back to the lobby, looking somewhat perturbed.

"Come with me, Hastings wants to see you."

As we walked down the hallway I heard Hastings ask Evelyn if we could use her office for a few minutes. She agreed, and went into another office down the hall.

"All right, Mr. Matthews. Enough of this charade. Where are the contents of this cylinder?"

Immediately I looked at Wallace. "I gave it to you."

Hastings responded sharply, "I want the contents from this cylinder!"

"Give me a break. I took the cylinder and handed it to Walleye here, pointing at Wallace.

"When the hell could I have taken anything out of it? Your men were right there."

Wallace told me to keep my voice down while Hastings was staring at the empty cylinder deep in thought. While he was silent for the moment, I looked around the room. I felt a strange familiarity. It was the paintings hanging on the walls. I drew to the one where a man and a woman sat on a blanket, having a picnic by a river. The woman had a warm smile on her face as she looked at the man sitting with her, whose face wasn't shown. The caption under the painting read; "The Look of Love." It had to have been Willow and Web.

While I was absorbed by the painting I heard Hastings tell Wallace to contact the pilot and tell him we'll be taking off within the hour. I tuned out what else they were saying because I was drawn to another painting. It was dark, mostly grey and some black. It was of a man with his back turned, standing near the edge of a cliff, looking slightly over his shoulder to the left. It depicted him looking over a great distance. I looked at the caption. It blew me away. It read, "I envy the wind. It has no memory of where it's been."

There could be only one explanation to this. This had to have been Willow's office. I wanted to take a closer look at the other paintings, but lingering here wasn't on Hastings schedule. He made it clear we needed to be on our way so he and I could talk more in depth regarding the absence of information they were expecting, and as he put it, I was suppose to deliver. As he motioned for us to leave, I thought it odd that the name plate on the desk had been turned face down. I turned it right side up, and couldn't believe what I saw. It stopped cold in my tracks. I looked at Hastings and he knew what I was thinking. The name plate read, "Evelyn W. Stone."

Coincidence? It couldn't be! Might she be Web and Willow's

daughter? I had to find out. She was sitting in the office down the hall. I ran out and rushed to her office, and blurted out, "I think I know your father."

She looked quite surprised, then replied, "You must be mistaken, my father died in Vietnam before I was born."

Just then Wallace came in, grabbed my arm, and hauled me out of the office. Evelyn rushed to the door and asked what was going on? I shoved Wallace hard into the wall, and he fell to the floor. I turned to Evelyn, and hurriedly asked, "Was his name Hudson Stone?"

She was visibly shaken. Her voice quivered as she answered, "Yes, yes it was."

"Mr. Matthews!" Hastings voice echoed loudly in the hallway. "It's time we were leaving, now!"

"Wait, please just a minute!" Evelyn pleaded. "Do you Agents know something about my father?"

Hastings beat me to the draw. "Excuse me Miss Stone. I'm afraid Mr. Matthews has some issues he knows better than to address at this time. I apologize for the ambiguity. Please accept our thanks for your help and co-operation."

Hastings gave me a look that spoke volumes. I knew I had to leave without saying another word. I glanced over my shoulder as we walked out. Evelyn stood motionless in the hallway. She looked like a lost lamb with no family anywhere to be found. Her eyes were pleading, yearning for some answers. She reached out her hand to me, but I couldn't do a thing. One day I said to myself, I will make this up to her.

The car ride to the airport was a silent one. Not a word was spoken. When we had taken off in the jet, Hastings expressed his frustration.

"Mr. Matthews. You seem to forget there is a time to speak and a time to be quiet. Don't mix them up again."

"Give me a break. That was Web's daughter, and you expect me to ignore that?"

"That was an unacceptable stunt you pulled back at the museum. Don't pull anymore stunts. Besides, I don't like wild goose chases. Never have. Did you forget you only get so many chances at bat? Right now you're at strike two. Your last chance will come after we land."

"What now? I've told you what I know. I can't explain anymore than I have!"

"Then explain this to me. What can you tell me about a Mr. Franklin D. Rose?"

Great! My last ace was gone. They knew about the cabin.

"I thought you told me one shouldn't ask questions they know the answers to?" I asked.

"Who says I know the answer to my question?"

I didn't answer. It wasn't any use. I asked what he wanted from me.

"We're going to that cabin right now. You better hope we find something."

Once we got off the plane, I asked to call Lily, and again told abruptly no. The four of us drove to the cabin, where we were joined by six more "Agents". I feared Web's secrets would be in their hands in short order.

The "Agents" that joined us brought sledgehammers and wrecking bars. They were going to trash the cabin looking for Web's secrets. Once inside Hastings sent them to various parts of the cabin, to search and destroy as he put it. I had to stop them.

"Wait! Don't! Please don't. Let me show you." I went over to the picture and did my magic with the wall panel. Sure enough the panel opened and I told them what they wanted was inside. Hastings went in, pulled the string, and the light came on. All was silent. Wallace joined him in the small room. I went to the doorway and looked in. I was about to be enlightened.

Hastings stood in there looking closely at the walls. I stood there in disbelief. The walls were all bare except for one. On the one wall was a large brown envelope. It had something written on it. I stepped closer. It was a name. I was experiencing yet another unfolding of events I never saw coming. The envelope had the name "Porter" written on it.

"So just what exactly is this suppose to be?" Hastings asked

"I don't know. That wasn't there the last time I looked in here."

He took the envelope off the wall. He made no attempt to open it. One of the missing pieces of this puzzle had just surfaced. There was only one logical answer. I turned and saw all the "Agents" staring at me. All I did was smile. A mile wide smile. This puzzle piece that showed up was very significant. My eyes locked with Hastings'. He knew now that I knew. There was only one answer to what happened in this room, the microfilm missing at the museum, and the empty canister in Web's garden. Web had retrieved everything. They didn't capture him that night. That was all a ruse. He had outsmarted them again.

Hastings told his men they done here. Wallace and Philips gave me their customary look of disgust as they walked out. Hastings stayed in the cabin. He sat down on the couch and motioned for me to sit in the chair. He didn't speak right away. He set the envelope on the coffee table and began looking around the room. His customary wringing of his gloved hands was the only sound to be heard. I wasn't sure what to expect.

"Well Mr. Matthews."

"Call me Quint, I'm not that old."

"That is a strange name. Where ever did your mother come up with that name?"

"Named me after a blacksmith on an old TV western, *Gunsmoke*. But somehow why do I think you already knew that?"

"Well, Quint, there still are two very sharp tools in the box. On occasion one appears to be a tad sharper than the other. I will have to concede on that point. Nevertheless, like my friend, Atticus, I'll be straight with you. I can't give up the search for Hudson, I think you must know that?"

"That's the first time you've called him Hudson."

He didn't respond. Speaking of names, I had a question for him.

"Why aren't you opening the envelope?"

"It's not for me, it's for someone named Porter."

"Give it to me and I'll open it."

"That won't be necessary. I'll have our lab check it out."

"Are you afraid of what might be inside?"

"In my profession fear doesn't enter the picture."

I lunged forward and grabbed the envelope. He didn't even stir.

"There may be fingerprint evidence on that, so hand it back to me."

Still holding the envelope, I thought about what he said. I realized, why the gloves.

"Your gloves. You never take them off. You're making sure that you never leave your prints anywhere, right?"

Again, no response.

"So let me guess. You make sure that your prints aren't found anywhere but I'll bet that inside this envelope is a picture. A picture of you. A picture you need to destroy because like your prints, you don't want any evidence that you exist, right? Enter, The Groundskeeper A.K.A Hudson. He took pictures of most every assignment to confirm the erasing of the intended mark."

I knew I was going out on a limb but the more I went out on it the clearer things became. I had to inch a little further.

"I wouldn't be surprised if the picture in this envelop is one of you on the ground with three slugs in your chest."

"Young man, let me remind you, you don't hold any aces in this game, I hold them all. And while you may try to be a one eyed jack, my house of cards will never come down. You're overlooking the issue at hand. You've had three chances at bat, and you've struck out. You failed to deliver."

I cringed as he reached in his coat and pulled out his gun.

"Fine, I get the point. Here's your damn envelope." I tossed it back on the coffee table. He reached in his other pocket and took out something else. Oh hell! A Silencer!

"Come on man, you don't need to do this."

Undaunted, he slowly attached the silencer to the gun.

"I truly hoped it wouldn't have had to come to this. But you haven't given me much choice."

My heart raced as he aimed the gun at me. Three shots whistled with a puffing sound. I grabbed my chest and breathed in. I didn't feel any pain. I looked up at him. The gun was still pointed in my direction.

"Those were three warning shots. The first warning shot was to remind you that if you want to stay alive, you're not to reveal anything you know, to anyone. The second shot was to remind you, you know, 'Every breath you take, every move you make', we'll be watching you. The third shot was to remind you to forget Hudson Stone. Move on with your life. I'll need your word on this."

I was still recovering from the shots. I looked at the wall behind me and he added another reminder.

"I suggest you don't repair the bullet holes in the wall, so there will be that constant reminder when I'm gone."

"Obviously you have my word. I don't have a choice, as usual."

He reached for the envelope on the table.

"So tell me. Was I right about the envelope?" I asked.

"What was it I told you about questions you know the answers to?"

"But how did you survive three in the chest, especially where you were, so far from a hospital?"

"Let just say the we had very unique bulletproof vests, that contained a layer of red fluid to simulate bleeding. I was the first to try one out. We have a significant number of devices that will never reach store shelves."

"What don't you guys have?" I asked.

"Hudson M. Stone."

"Wasn't it your people who trained him to disappear?"

"And that it was."

"Did it ever occur to you that he just wanted to be left alone? Can't you just give it up. I mean like he's an old man. He's no threat to you."

"As long as he's breathing, he's a threat to us."

Still breathing. Those words reminded me that I was still breathing because Hastings chose to let me live. I felt I needed to thank him.

"By the way, I know that I'm still breathing only because you have allowed it to be so. Thank you for that."

"Well truth be known, I owed Hudson. The only way I could repay him is to spare someone close to him like yourself."

"What do you mean, you owed him?"

"Just a little matter on an assignment, back in '72. To be precise, May 2nd. Time was up for Mr. J. Edgar Hoover. Just before I administered his injection he pulled a gun from under his pillow. I didn't see it in time, but Hudson did. He wrestled it away from the little bastard and held him down. I injected him, and as he went into cardiac arrest, he slid off the bed onto the floor, and died right there. That's where they found him next morning, at the side of his bed."

He stood up walked over to me, and held out his hand to shake mine. Unexpected to say the least. Reluctantly I obliged. Still, I felt the need to inch a little further on the same limb.

"I have just one more question. How do I get a hold of you, if I need to? You must have some office or somewhere that I can call?"

"We don't have a phone number."

"Well, what about the name of your organization?"

"We don't have a name. We don't have an address, we don't have an office. We basically don't exist."

"How can you not have a name for your organization?"

"Quite simple. Having no name, means there's nothing to trace, nothing to connect us with, no one to track down. Nowhere to start looking. That's the way we want it."

"Kind of adds new meaning to a 'Secret Society.'"

"And that it does. However, if you want to get my attention, I think you know the quickest way."

"What's that?"

"Same way you got it before. Just type in your search for, 'The Three Jimmies.'"

CHAPTER TWENTY

Seven years later—December 2006
A year can bring many changes. Seven years brings many more. However to this day I've kept my word to Hastings and haven't shared anything with anyone, especially Lily. I need to keep her safe, along with our son Hudson, and our little precious, Evelyn. I've found a joy that's nearly complete. All that is missing is Web. As the years have slipped by I don't think of him as much as I used to. Time has a way of easing memories, even the good ones. But I do think of him every time I drive the Yenko, every time I step in our backyard, and every time we go to the cabin. When the memories revisit me, I still think of him as Web, even though that's not his real name. Perhaps one day, I will share my silent memories. Lily would be the only one I would want to share them with. Then, many years from now, I would like to tell Hudson about his great grandfather; a very wise, brave, and unselfish man.

There are times when we're at the cabin, when I can't sleep, that I'll stoke up the fire, sit on the couch, and think of him. I'll listen to the classical music he loved so much, Bach and others. I still wonder what happened the night he got out of the car at Green Road. Here it is some seven years later, and still no answers. I often wonder if his heart gave out on him after all he's been through. Some of our greatest pains come from the unknown answers to questions that haunt us. Not knowing is something I wish I could change. Then again, life is like that, there are things we so desperately want to change, but it's not to be.

I've never encountered Hastings since that last meeting at the cabin. I haven't seen any of his men for at least two or three years. But I know they're watching, listening, monitoring. Every time I use the phone, computer, go on a trip, I know there's no eluding them. I've learned to live with it. I once thought of going to Hayden, Arizona, wondering if Web referred to it as some kind of clue about his future whereabouts. It would have a long shot at best. The reality is of course, that if he's still alive, he could be living anywhere. Wherever that might be I'm sure he'd be caring for some beautiful garden, and have a house near a stream with lots of willow trees.

I never did join the Police force. Web's take on that was all so true. Corruption knows no limit. It's all around us. Along with greed, pride and ambition, it makes for a fearsome foursome.

"Quint, can you get the door, I'm bathing Evelyn."

I didn't even hear the bell. I was so deep in thought. I answered the door and a postal worker greeted me.

"Mr. Quint Matthews?"

"Yes, that's me."

"I have a delivery for you. The box was at the post office for a few days. You'll notice there's some kind of Customs Inspection label on the side, so the box was opened and resealed. Just sign here to accept."

"Thank you." I brought the parcel into the living room.

Customs Inspection? Yeah, right. Thanks again guys for respecting my privacy. The return address was some book club, which I wouldn't know anything about anyway. Lily probably had it sent to me. She always telling me I should read more books. I opened the box. It was a dictionary. Why would she send me a dictionary? There must be three or four around here as it is. Likely she hopes it will increase my word power.

I set the dictionary on the table while I waited for Lily to finish with Evelyn. As I walked out of the room, I stopped. It just struck me. I went back into the living room. It wasn't just any dictionary it was a *Webster's Dictionary*. A silent old memory revisited. I remember Web telling me, "Look me up in *Webster's*." Could it be? Could this possibly be from Web? I grabbed the dictionary thinking, where would I look? I checked inside the cover, front and back. I tipped it over and shook it, hoping some note would fall out. Nothing. I looked for a folded page, some kind of marking, but still nothing. I leafed through it, to check for any writing on a page, any page. Still nothing. Maybe it's a certain word. Where to look? Web! That's it. I'll look under the word, "Web." I flipped through the "W"s, again and again, but there was no word, "Web." Wait a minute. Page four thirty-four then page four thirty-seven. Strange I thought. Page four thirty-five and four thirty-six were missing. The word "Web" would have been on page four thirty-five, but there were no tear marks or anything. Then I saw it. Close to the binding was a small remnant of the page still attached. This page four thirty-five had been very carefully cut out of the book.

I leaned back and smiled. This was unbelievable. I checked the postage stamp. It was mailed nine days ago. What a sly old fox. He was still alive! He slipped another one by them. Who would have thought to check the book for a missing page? This was fantastic! For over thirty years he had outsmarted them. I wondered from where he sent it? I checked the post office stamp, and the parcel was mailed from, looks like Viola, Kansas. Viola, Kansas? Viola. Viola. I remembered something he said once, "Violas should be at the center of every orchestra." He had to have sent it from there for a reason. But why? Why from there?

I took an atlas from the shelf and opened it to a map of the U.S. I could see Wichita, Kansas City, but no Viola. I turned to a map of the state of Kansas and there it was, southwest of Wichita, right in the middle of nowhere. Come to think of it, the middle. I looked at the previous map and located the spot. Now I knew. He sent it from a location smack dab in the middle of the United States. What a guy! He sent it from there, because he could go in any direction, and "they" wouldn't know where to start looking for him.

The time had finally come. I called out to Lily.

"Lily, can you come down to the living room?"

"I'll be right there. I'm just putting Evelyn in her crib."

"Put on a pot of coffee. We're going to have a very long talk."

To be continued...